THE SCORE

In desperate circumstances a man
and a woman come together for
the purposes of survival. Always
relentlessly pursued, they set out
on their journey; find happiness and
deep sorrow, betray one another and
others but somehow keep on going.
Children come and are loved, but
vanish again, before their final goal
is reached. But there, 'the score' is
settled.

JANE MORELL

THE SCORE

Complete and Unabridged

LINFORD
Leicester

First published in Great Britain in 1989 by
Robert Hale Limited
London

First Linford Edition
published 1996
by arrangement with
Robert Hale Limited
London

British Library CIP Data

Morell, Jane
    The score.—Large print ed.—
    Linford romance library
    1. English fiction—20th century
    2. Large type books
    I. Title
    823.9'14 [F]

    ISBN 0–7089–7971–8

Published by
F. A. Thorpe (Publishing) Ltd.
Anstey, Leicestershire

Set by Words & Graphics Ltd.
Anstey, Leicestershire
Printed and bound in Great Britain by
T. J. Press (Padstow) Ltd., Padstow, Cornwall

This book is printed on acid-free paper

Prologue

1969

THEY had been following the insurgents all day: the third since picking up their trail. Were now in country which none of them knew: the southern deserts, very sparsely populated, on the edge of the Empty Quarter. Came to the village around 4.30 in the afternoon and knew that they had to go in and search it, in case any of the men they were after had holed up there. A small village, ringed by high mud-brick walls to keep the drifting sand at bay, its groves of date-palms behind them clearly visible from a long way off.

Three hundred yards from the gate the major, driving the lead Land Rover, slowed down and stopped. When the other two LRs came up beside him, gave his orders: the lieutenant to head east, round the village, looking for other entrances, exits, and when he found them, as he surely would, to halt, deploy his men and keep them covered; the sergeant to make for that rise, over there — he pointed — from which he should be able to command a view both of the village and the desert for many miles around; to wait there until sent for, or until he spotted anything which might be of interest to them. Meanwhile, he himself and his lot would go in. If he didn't come out again within the hour they would please come looking for him, taking appropriate precautions. Understood?

Understood. The two LRs took off in opposite directions, at speed, trailing the usual clouds of dust. He gave them time, five minutes, and then motored to the gate and drew up before it. Cautioned his men, before he got down, that there was no question but that, to this village, they came for the moment in peace, and that they should behave themselves accordingly. Until such time as events might appear to justify a different approach, when he and no one else would give the order. Having commanded Baluchi troops for some years now he knew something of their strengths and weaknesses: hard men, fearless, but liable to react unpredictably in unfamiliar circumstances unless they knew exactly what was required of them.

He went to the gate, solid teak, brass studded, and hammered upon it with a stone, his four troopers, in battledress and heavily armed, at his back. Not surprised that they had seen no one so far and that no one had come out to meet them: in high summer and at this hour all sensible people kept to the shade and shelter of their homes until it became absolutely imperative to do something else.

At the third knock a small panel in the gate was opened. A dark bearded face, eyes bleary with sleep, confronted him. With it he exchanged the usual greetings and enquiries, asked permission to enter the village. No problem, no hesitation at all: the dark face disappeared, there came the sounds of rusted bolts being drawn back and of a bar being lifted, and then a door in the big gate was thrown wide. They went through, one by one, the major leading; found themselves in a dusty sun-drenched open space with low mud-walled houses about it shaded by mature palm-trees: apart from the old 'watchman', a few goats the only living creatures in view. Then came people, a party of men, young and old; they appeared in a broad alleyway leading towards them from the heart of the village, and approached without hurry.

Carefully the major ran his eye over them as they came towards him, but they were villagers, all of them, that and nothing else, he was fairly certain of it.

A tall man in the lead: the Mukhtar,

doubtless, in his late thirties, perhaps, bearded, hawk-faced, with a cast in one eye: he extended his hand in greeting, without smiling, and the major shook hands while, again, the usual polite enquiries, as to health and circumstances, were exchanged. At the Headman's side stood a young boy, lithe, handsome, perhaps fourteen years old who, in due turn, was introduced as the Headman's eldest child and only son. The boy's eyes, alight with intelligence and curiosity, openly studying this 'Sah'b' now arrived so unexpectedly in their midst — his sweat-stained uniform and well-worn equipment — roving on to encompass the foreign soldiery at his back, their watchful bearing and gleaming weapons: beings, all five of them, from another world, one that he would some day know something of, God willing.

The Mukhtar offered refreshment and, as custom demanded, the major accepted. The two men walked together across the little square and entered the secluded alleys of the village, a throng of villagers accompanying them now, the four Baluchi troopers bringing up the rear. The risks involved in what they were doing not negligible, the major knew it, but ones that could only have been avoided by employing much harsher tactics altogether, from the start, for which, thus far, he had seen no justification at all. So be it: he and the Mukhtar walked on, in silence, as gradually the conviction grew in him that in this village there was nothing to be feared. Nor would they find any trace of what they were looking for, that was a near-certainty also, but never mind, such delays as this in their pursuit had to be accepted with good grace. At least, perhaps, they might obtain news.

Truly, news, some of it very useful. After the major, the village elders, the Headman, had all seated themselves on mats in the village majlis, and after the boy — his name Selim — had brought in and served coffee, placed glasses of clean water and trays of spiced dates to hand, he broached the reason for his visit: a group of four men, two of them foreign Arabs, in a big Toyota, had they passed this way?

But yes, the Headman said immediately, the day before, near sundown: they had stopped for an hour at the village, taken food, bought two chickens; then left.

"Which way did they go?" the major asked. Before him the boy Selim knelt on one knee, beaked brass pot in hand, ready to refill his tiny cup, and he held it out, smiling into the lad's eyes.

"To the east," the Headman said. "Towards the sunrise and the sea."

Four hundred miles, to the sea, the major thought. Pray God they caught up with them before they got that far: a hellish long way, and hellish going, most of it. He looked round, asking, "Did anyone get a look at their vehicle?"

For the first time the Headman smiled, briefly, and waved a hand at his son now filling someone else's cup down the line. Said, "I did not, but the boy did, I think."

The youth rose to his feet. Spoke up without shyness when the major looked at him. Said, "They would not let me get close, they were rude and told me to go away, but I saw, yes, a few things — "

"Petrol? They had spare cans with them?"

"Three, four, in the back. But maybe one or two were for water."

"Very likely," the major said. And even if they did have *four* cans, full ones, the vehicle they had still could not carry them much more than a further couple of hundred miles. "Do you know anything about engines, ya-Selim?" he asked quietly. "What did theirs sound like? Did it sound in good condition?"

"Not good," the boy said at once. "It is old and much used. It has not been looked after well."

Again the major smiled, liking what

he saw of this boy very much. Said, "You know quite a bit about vehicles, I can see that — how did you learn?"

"I go to Kamil, to visit my relatives. My uncle there, he has two jeeps, and I learn from him. Sometimes we go together, hunting, in the desert."

"May God grant you good fortune, always," the major said.

★ ★ ★

That night they camped outside the village, a quarter of a mile from it, in the desert. The major and the lieutenant had been invited in to take food after sundown, and this they did, returning to camp, sleepy and replete, not long after nine o'clock. A cloudless night with no moon, the heavens awash with stars, so that you could believe that you were indeed in the presence of infinity.

The Baluchis had a fire going, a small one, and sat round it in a ring, all except two of their number who

9

were on guard. While the lieutenant went to his sack, the major hunkered down with the men for a while, let them speak their minds with him there to listen, if there was anything to say. A small example of the care he took, that these men, foreigners like himself in a strange land, a long way from home, should occasionally have the opportunity to air their views and have their questions answered. Trust, devotion, between officers and men, of enormous importance in a situation such as theirs. Tomorrow, or the next day, if the fates were kind, they would go into action against a small group of well-armed and desperate men: when that happened the quality of the relationship which he had with those under his command might make all the difference.

The sergeant, a veteran of Imphal and Kohima, spoke first, as was his right. Asked the major's plans for the morning.

He had already told them they would

be off again at first light. Now, gave them a further detail. "Kamil," he said. "It's possible 'the Adoo' have changed their minds and are now heading over that way — in the hope of obtaining petrol, or another vehicle. So the lieutenant-Sah'b will go to Kamil tomorrow — "

"Unlikely," the sergeant said, and several of the men shook their heads also. "Those 'soors'" — meaning the enemy — "they are themselves from the coast. They will keep going in that direction, in the hope of meeting up with friends."

"I think so too," the major said. "Yes." But added a warning note, in all seriousness. "It is also possible that being short of fuel, they will turn and fight, in a day or two, any time, or that their vehicle may break down, and we should be prepared for that."

"They may not be far away now," one of the soldiers said quietly.

"And if they are going to attack they

11

will surely seek to do so by night," said another.

"Very probably," the major said. He smiled around, and went on, "Which is one very good reason for the watch being strictly maintained during the hours of darkness, is it not?"

Nods of agreement all round: the sergeant's steely eye singling out those men, already detailed off, who would be on duty that night. Shortly afterwards the major bid them goodnight and went his way. Had a quiet whisky in the tent which he and the lieutenant shared, without waking his junior officer, before turning in. Slept almost immediately, his thoughts always, last thing, of his wife and daughter, back home. Three months to go, only, until his next leave.

★ ★ ★

Rifle-fire, in the night, single shots, a rapid burst, then silence. He was out of his tent, stumbling, regaining his feet, as the lights from the LRs came on, lighting up the desert round camp for a hundred yards on all sides. There was nothing to be seen, out there, but the camp roused, the sergeant shouting orders, men crawling from their tents, rifles and machine-pistols in hand. Movement, heavy breathing, the clatter of rifle bolts, as the men deployed, taking cover in the shadow and protection of the Land Rovers, their weapons raised, seeking something to shoot at, if the order were given. But nothing to be seen, within range of the lights, flat desert, empty, a little camel-thorn, that was all. The major's mind registered the feel of the night air, cool, clammy; it wasn't far off dawn, he thought. Beside him, the sergeant snarled, "Mirza, Bakhti — *idha ao!*"

The two men who had been on watch crawled over, and made their report, breathing hard. Three men, they said: shadows in the night, over there, maybe fifty yards from camp, to the south; he, Mirza, had fired, warning shots, to miss, as instructed.

"Sure? Totally sure — men?" the major snapped.

Yes, sure. No doubt at all. He, Mirza had good night-vision, as the Sahib knew.

He nodded, and gave his orders. Everyone to stand to, until first light, the LRs' headlights to be left on; Sher, the cook, to get hot tea going; no one to move around; everyone to *keep down*, behind cover as far as possible, until they could see better what they were doing. The Adoo, if they had been Adoo, out there, could have rifles with them and he didn't want anyone picked off from long range.

Gradually the time passed, and the light grew. In the silent camp men and officers waited, in small groups by the three Land Rovers, their weapons within reach. Tea was brought, hot and sweet with condensed milk, served into enamel mugs from the kettle; occasionally a man crawled away to relieve himself in privacy; otherwise no one broke cover. As soon as increasing daylight permitted the lights were switched off, and shortly after that the major and four men went out into the desert, searching for tracks.

Found them, easily enough, in approximately the place Private Mirza said they would: fifty yards out, in a southerly direction from camp: a confused pattern, made by two or more men, barefooted. They had approached camp from the direction of the village, the grey walls of which, and the palm-trees behind, could now be seen clearly enough through the mists of morning; they had begun crawling on all fours towards camp, the scuff-marks of their progress not hard to make out in patches of soft sand — had then been shot at and had turned tail and run. Who they had been, no indication, carefully though everyone searched; what had been their purpose in approaching camp, also no clue. After the major had seen what little there was to see, he led his men back to camp, to have breakfast. Thinking that after breakfast he might follow the tracks of the running men to see where they led, using the LRs to save time, but doubting whether there was any useful purpose to be served. Better to forget the incident and get on, perhaps: if those had been Adoo, in the night, they were far away by now.

It was while he and the lieutenant were breakfasting together, on coffee, hard-boiled eggs and stale bread, that the sergeant came to tell him that people, many people, were coming from the village in the direction of camp: why, he didn't know but, maybe, from the look of them, their silence, there was something wrong. He got up immediately, went to stand by his own LR, from where he could see them; then quickly got glasses from under the dash and focused them on the crowd he could see coming.

The Mukhtar in the lead, carrying a body in his arms, a thin body, a young body, arms and head dangling, lifeless.

For a few seconds the major's mind refused to credit what he saw, and then he murmured, aloud but to himself, "Jesus Christ!" He had *told* them, he had made a *point* of it, the evening before, over food: warned the Mukhtar and asked him to spread the word among his people: that their camp *must not* be approached during the hours of darkness, on any pretext whatsoever; that no villager should come anywhere near it, because he and his men were on active service and there would be armed sentries posted with orders to shoot; and this the Mukhtar had given his solemn promise that he would do. Because, however good a man's night-vision might be, and even though his orders were to shoot to miss in the first instance, and he followed them, yet — an accident could happen. Goddammit, a young boy, a good young boy, what had he been up to, and why had he disobeyed? Never mind, there might be a dozen reasons and none of them mattered, now.

17

His voice rough with emotion the major ordered his men to stand to, had the sergeant mount the heavy machine-gun in the back of one of the Land Rovers. But, in truth, the mood of the crowd approaching did not appear hostile, as far as he could see; they didn't have weapons — such as they might possess — with them. Their mood was one of sadness and mourning, that was all.

Part One

Choices

Part One

Choices

1

1989

THE situation was tense and had been for some time. Three hundred miles away in the capital the old Sultan lay dying and what would happen after he had gone was anyone's guess. A coup d'état was highly likely and if the wrong side came out on top in that, then the few Brits left in the country could be in serious trouble. This was known, contingency plans had been sanctioned and made ready, but until the event or events took place, if they did, there was little more to be done. People went on with their work.

The day's stint over, after a late lunch in the mess and a siesta, she followed her normal pattern took a towel, a book, and walked away from camp to a line of low bergs three or four hundred yards away. Climbed to the crests and, in a secluded hollow among the rocks, took her clothes off and sunbathed. She would do this for an hour or so, reading and thinking, then do her exercises; then dress and run for half an hour in the desert, before returning to camp. She had a lean exciting body — so she had been told often enough — and liked to keep it looking good. Her name: Elyane Mash'al, a black-eyed tow-headed girl of Lebanese extraction, though she had never once actually set foot in that doomed country, by inclination and training a scientist — beginning to establish herself in the field of carbon-dating — dedicated, single, her Arabic as near fluent as made no difference.

But there were other sides to her also. Of course, other sides.

This day she followed her routine most of the way through, but did not return to camp immediately. Sat resting on a rock, half a mile out, while the sun inched down towards the horizon: letting the desert, the mile upon mile of emptiness, get to her, envelop her, talk to her in its own way, as she had done a number of times before. Talk to her (among other things) of the many faces of hardship and suffering, of a people — who since time immemorial had chosen, or been compelled, to make such places as this their home — who had nurtured in themselves whatever it took to endure, and survive. A cruel people, in a cruel land, much closer to the eternal verities, she believed, than herself: at first hand she knew little of their lives, but had read much and divined more. Respected, and feared, in them all that she had lost and could never have again, a different (and subtler) kind of freedom, soon to be banished from the face of the earth.

Far away to the north she could just make out the high peaks of the Jebel Hajjar beginning to appear like spectres above the haze, yellow-fanged in slanting sunlight. At this time of day, for an hour or so only, they became visible, drawing the eyes to them almost hypnotically, if you knew where to look. She had never been up there, in the mountains, but would go one day, God willing —

But sweat: the tracksuit she was wearing clung to her body, and suddenly she had had enough, felt mentally and physically drained. Needed a shower now and, more vitally, salt tablets and a long cool drink. So gathered up her things and began to walk back, her sneakers making little sound over windswept sand. Came to the wadi — grey-dry at this time of year — and crossed it; entered the belt of acacia trees on the far side. Crickets sang in that place, and occasionally camels — surly grumbling beasts to be watched, from a safe distance, with real pleasure — came from God knew where to graze the young greenery. No camels today, however, and 'the site' beyond empty: the three third-millenium grave-mounds in a line which were the main reason for the presence of the team she was with in this part of the country. All three mounds were being worked on, each had its tripod lifting-gear poised above it, and there were picks, shovels, barrows left leaning against piles of rubble and labelled stone nearby.

She made her way between 'Ayoun 1' and 'Ayoun 2', the ancient man-made tumuli both nearly twice her height; then, as the camp-site came into view, slowed her pace a moment, before going on. To her left, thirty yards off, a man in shorts and open shirt sat cross-legged on the ground like an Arab, waiting for her. Waiting for her? Perhaps.

* * *

Andersen, he was called, Jack Andersen, in fact she knew him hardly at all: he was something of a loner, she guessed, like herself. In addition he had only joined their team on arrival in the country a couple of months before — deputed to look after them by the Consulate in the capital — and spent a lot of his time elsewhere, not at the dig itself. A man in his mid-thirties, not tall but very strongly built, with a certain latent authority about him that she hadn't met too often before (he had been a professional soldier, once, she had heard, which might well, she supposed, have something to do with it) who came and went among them, kept them supplied, liaised on their behalf with government departments, and so on, but otherwise played little part. A good-looking guy in his way, very fair, his face a trifle world-weary but friendly enough, with good lines, the eyes perceptive and resourceful; also sometimes revealing a warmth towards her which she found no difficulty in taking in her stride.

After greeting each other, and shaking hands, they walked on together, back towards camp: the laagered trailers and portakabins in the distance, the two water-bowsers under their awnings, the generating plant whose scarcely-muted racket had become part of their existence. In his own time, and breaking a small silence between them thereby, he put it to her, without preamble, the reason he had come out to meet her. "Your people over there." He pointed with his chin. "They're taking all this, what may be about to happen in this country, a little too casually, I think." His voice low-pitched, always, very seldom raised.

"You think we should be doing more? What can we do?"

"You should be better prepared," he said. "Ready, at five minutes notice, to get in your jeeps and get the hell out, back to the capital — "

"Leaving all our equipment, all our gear, just like that?" She shook her head, raised a hand to brush trailing hair from her eyes. "It isn't on. Not unless things get a great deal worse."

He was silent again, for a moment or

two. Then said, "If anything is going to happen, believe me, it could happen very fast."

"Out here?"

He nodded. "Yes, even out here. Perhaps," he added, "more especially 'out here'."

"So why tell me?" she asked curiously. "What does Peter say?" Peter was the leader of their team, a Cambridge don of international reputation; she had been sleeping with him for some time: an almost entirely physical commitment, on her side at least. He was getting round to asking her to marry him, she suspected and, if he did, was frankly torn two ways as to what her response should be. He had, when she thought about it, so much going for him that she wanted — would, without question, be supportive of her desire to continue with her work — but the prospect meant little to her nevertheless, was a challenge she could do without, now, and probably for several years yet. When she did marry, and if, the thing to do was do it properly, she believed — kids, the lot — and she was by no means ready for all that at the present time. Would, if she accepted him, make him a bloody-awful wife, therefore, and store up limitless trouble for herself.

"Peter's a good man," Andersen said carefully, looking away. "Doubtless in his own line a very good man. For all that he's been around, though, he's never been in a situation quite like this one, I think. Nor in a *country* quite like this." He halted beside her, held out his hand, compelling her to halt with him. Stared at her, putting what he had to say on the line, and demanding that she listen. "He sees the work that you're doing getting results, reaching fruition, and he wants nothing to interfere with your rhythm, your concentration. He says you're Brits, foreign nationals, here with the consent and blessing of the government in being and protected by international agreements. He cannot really believe, I suppose, even in this day and age, that anything *can* happen to you. Just as you do, also, he says that some of your equipment is highly valuable, paid for by the British taxpayer and various foundations worldwide, and that you cannot think of abandoning it except in the last resort. He shrugged and made a face, before concluding, "All fine, all understood — up to a point. The fact remains that the next government of this country could well turn out to be a lot less friendly to you than the present one has been. More importantly, before that government has time to establish itself, there will very likely be an intervening period of chaos."

"But, the Embassy?" she asked. "They have their finger on the pulse, don't they? Peter's in touch with them every day, I know. Surely they would warn us, in good time?" She turned and walked on, head down, and he fell into step beside her once again.

"Embassies are not in the business of sowing alarm and confusion," he said shortly. "Not until it becomes absolutely vital to do so." Quietly he went on, "I was there, day before yesterday, saw the First Secretary, and confirmed the arrangements they've made for you. As Peter has already told you, I think, they will send trucks to get you, and your gear, if things start to get rough. You will then proceed in convoy to the capital and when you get there an RAF Hercules will be standing by to fly you out. The only thing is that those trucks have a very long way to come and who knows what state the capital may be in by the time you finally arrive."

The camp-site wasn't far away now, but suddenly she felt very weary again, almost out on her feet. Held herself together by an effort of will and made for an ancient desert well a little way off the trail and sat down on the low parapet of mortared stone surrounding it. Sat there looking up at him, as he followed her over. Impressed, to some degree at any rate, by what he had had to say so far, that was undeniable — he did, after all, know this country a good deal better than any of the rest of them did. Thinking that almost certainly he and Peter had had a stand-up row, quite recently, during which her lover had chosen not to listen to him, had waved aside his fears for their safety as premature, and dismissed any suggestions that he may have made as both needless and counterproductive, at least for the time being: a rebuff which he, Andersen, was by no means disposed to take lying down. So he had come to her — why, she wondered, because she was by some way the most junior of the team gathered together here at Ayoun and her influence, therefore, even with Peter, fairly negligible. A suspicion growing in the mind that this man, who now stood over her, watching her in his turn, had something else he wanted to say, perhaps of greater significance, at least to his own way of thinking, than anything he had vouchsafed so far: something, maybe, that he'd felt unable even to put to Peter, or suspected that Peter might not understand.

"Hell, I'm sorry," he said suddenly. "You're dead beat and I'm keeping you — "

She shook her head. "It doesn't matter."

"The last thing I want is for all of you to be going around from now on expecting the worst. The worst may not happen. Peter may easily be right."

"But you don't think so?"

"No, I don't."

"Why? Truly, why?"

He moved abruptly and sat down beside her on the narrow wall of the old well. A closeness between them now that had never been there before: now that she had shown herself willing to go on listening to him. A physical 'call' also, brief but recognisable, which took her very much by surprise. Seriously, he said, "You've been to Kamil, haven't you?"

The regional capital, forty miles

distant, a very outback town and admin centre, hardly more than a big village: she had indeed been there a couple of times, had bought a length of brocade at one of the Indian dukas near the old market. She nodded and said, "Yes, I've been there."

"But you've never met the Wali, have you? The Regional Governor?"

"No."

"He's never visited you, out here," he said. "He ought to have done, but he hasn't."

"You've had dealings with him, though?" she prompted.

"Mm, two or three times in the past weeks." He paused. "But I've known *of* him, for several years."

"And — ?"

"He's like God in these parts."

"You — don't trust him?"

He looked away, grim-faced, eyes half-closed. "No, I don't trust him an inch. He's virulently anti-British, all foreigners for that matter, and he loathes Christians, for what reason I've no idea. On top of that his reputation hereabouts is vile, people fear him, but he is of the right family, the right tribe, and no one that I know of has ever dared suggest that he should be replaced."

"What's his name?"

"Seifuddin." He glanced at her. "He's a man in his late fifties, stooping, walks with a stick, never smiles. And his eyes — ." He shrugged and concluded, "You'll probably think me dim-witted if I tell you that when you're with him you feel, very strongly, that you're in the presence of evil."

She stared at him. If he felt the slightest embarrassment at what he had just said he didn't show it, nor did he seem inclined to retract or qualify one word. Again, and this time almost against her will, she was impressed. Hesitated, before saying, "You think, he might go for us? Is that what you're saying? If the situation were right?"

"Just that." He nodded. "If he believed he could get away with it."

35

She found it very difficult to accept, but then began to wonder. A real chill in her suddenly, a fear, of the unknown, that couldn't simply be dismissed out of hand. Making her say, after a time, "So, how can I help you? What is it you want me to do?"

He got to his feet and stood looking down at her again. "At 7.30 this evening," he said, "there's a get-together in the mess before supper: I've asked for it, and Peter's agreed — he couldn't really refuse. During that meeting he will call up the Embassy on the radio as he does around that time every day. They may have something to tell him or they may not — never mind — I still want to make an impassioned plea, to you all, that you should hold yourselves in readiness to make a quick run for it. To have places assigned in your available transport, the basic necessities ready packed, all vehicles tanked up and ready to go. And to put it to you that, from now on and until the situation sorts itself out, you should post armed guards round the camp, take turns at it yourselves, with me, day and night."

She nodded slowly. Then said, "And at this meeting, you want me to back you up? Is that it?"

"Yes. If you will? I want one person there, at least, who has some idea of the score."

"Why me?" she asked again. "Surely it might have been better — ?" She wasn't ducking the responsibility he was asking her to share, not by this time: merely curious, in the circumstances, that was all.

"Because," he said, "you are closer to this country than any of the others, I think. You 'sense' what can come out of it, and they don't."

"Me? I've only been here a couple of months. I know nothing."

"I think you do," he said. "In a way, sweet Elyane, it's in your blood. As it is in mine, after all these years."

She looked away, the endearment he had used giving her pause, not liking it one bit. Neither that, nor his presumption that he might 'know' her better than she did herself. The fact remained that, during the last twenty minutes or so, he had surely got through to her, this Andersen: shaken her, a little, and given her food for thought. *Not* her kind of man — that went without saying — but one whom, in present circumstances, it might pay them all to take a great deal more seriously than they had so far. So finally she said, "All right. I'll do what you ask."

He smiled, with obvious relief, and reached out his hands to help her to her feet. When she was up again, said, "Now, you've been wonderfully patient — let's get you in."

2

HE wanted her; had done for some time. Knew he was a fool; she was from another world, to which she was evidently devoted and would soon return, and in the meantime seemed perfectly content to bestow her sexual favours elsewhere. A thought he *hated*, because the apparent casualness of her liaison with Peter, if he read *her* feelings for the man aright, lessened her in his eyes. Nevertheless. Elyane Mash'al: 'Lina', they called her: an Arab girl who was yet, by domicile and upbringing, as Brit as they came; it was a combination, coupled with her striking looks and aura of self-reliance, which he found almost irresistible. He had known few women well in his time but those he had he had loved deeply, and been loved deeply in return, but for one

39

reason or another had never married. Life for him had meant service in too many places a long way off the beaten track and the women he had found in his travels, or during periods of leave in between, had all either been unwilling or unable in the last resort. Sadly, and in his heart he knew that he had been both lucky and unlucky, to date. And now there was this one, as unlike any other woman he had ever felt drawn to as it was possible to imagine, for whom — in the dark watches of the night — he suspected he might actually be prepared to lay down his life. Why? No answer, because up till and including today she had never — not by so much as a flicker of an eye — given him cause to believe that the chance might be there . . . Today *had* been different, however, a little and for the first time, under pressure of events. At least today, while they had talked together, for once in private, it had appeared to dawn on her at last that he might have something to offer; be a man who, because of his particular experience and talents, might conceivably have a vital role to play, however temporarily, in her life —

Cool, disconcerting creature that she was: he didn't actually *like* her too much.

After he had taken her back to the kabin she shared with the two other women on site, he set off to make a tour of camp. Something he had done many times before, for other reasons, but these days always with an eye on the horizon, on the layout, on the people, as and when they put in an appearance: looking for a sign, any sign, that everything was not quite as it should be. He was *not* responsible for this place and its security (Peter was) but could not but feel that way to some extent, in the circumstances —

Came first to the 'labour-lines', two kabins set a little apart from the others: both looked as though they had seen better days, and had lines of washing festooned between them. He mounted the steps of the first and put his head in

41

through the open doorway, murmuring a 'Salaam Aleikhom' as he did so. The lights and a/c were on but the racked bunks all empty and no one sat at the tables between, at which the men messed: Persians, eight in number, under a Palestinian overseer, they were very probably out in the desert at this hour, kicking a football about, as usual. He breathed in the smell, of cheap perfume, cheap cigarettes, eastern humanity and bedding, ran his eye over the tin trunks of belongings, the thobes hanging from pegs on the walls. They were a good lot, every single one of them, as far as he could tell, supplied by the Ministry in the capital: ruffianly to look at, maybe, but cheerful, willing, content with their pay and conditions, and there had never been any trouble among them that had reached his ears. They constituted, nevertheless, an unknown quantity in any emergency which had to be borne in mind. Foreigners, poor, in the country on visas revocable at any time, with dependent families and relatives elsewhere, they could be 'got at' in so many ways, and spent their day-off each week at Kamil, the provincial capital —

Next to their living-quarters, the kabin containing their cookhouse and ablutions; also, at the far end, the sleeping-room of the two Sri Lankan bearers, one an expert cook, who did for the whole camp. No likelihood of trouble with the Sri Lankans, he believed, none at all, both men of some education, both devoted to the 'Sah'bs' they worked for; Muslims, yes, but of a different persuasion from those to be found either side of the Gulf, who never, but never, strayed far from camp or their duties. His eyes roved on —

The nearest trailer/kabin to the 'labour lines', that of the team's mess, recreation room, commissariat, with kitchen at the back; the next Peter's quarters cum office, plus dark-room, plus radio-shack; beyond that the girls' dormitory; then that of the men; last,

43

and completing the circle, the kabin containing lab and general stores. Total: seven kabins, seven trailers, ten-fifteen yards separating each one, nothing but well-trodden sand in the ring across which they all faced. No one in sight now, not a soul: dusk was upon them and everyone was inside getting ready for the evening meal.

He walked across the ring, passed between men's kabin and lab, their a/cs jutting from their end walls, spitting and hissing, above his head, dripping water to form wet patches in the sand beneath them; stopped again. The vehicle-park fifty yards away. One long-wheel-base Land Rover, one Pajero, one Nissan Patrol, all showing signs of hard use but serviceable enough — Jones, the Australian, was a competent mechanic among other things — 44-gallon drums of fuel and oil in the shade of a kadjan shelter a little way from them. To have those vehicles, their gas, all spares, brought *inside* the circle of kabins, that was one of the first things he would insist on, at tonight's meeting; to leave them where they were was only asking for trouble. Those, and the two generators — the Nissan could haul them — which he could see further away, to his left. Madness, to leave them out there, whatever increase in racket it might mean to bring them in so close to everyones' living-quarters; madness to leave the big cable running from them across the sand to the camp-site, so exposed and vulnerable. It would mean a hell of a lot of work, some inconvenience and rewiring maybe, but it would have to be done, in the morning.

Across the desert now he could see the gang of Persians trailing back from their kickabout: they had a small 'field' marked out with stones and bits of angle-iron for posts down wadi a little way. Where they found the energy, after a hard day's work and in this heat, he didn't know, but more power to them; they were a tough breed. He turned away, thinking to go in now, shower and change.

But stopped at once, his eyes caught and held. Squatted down on his haunches and used his hands to shield his eyes and give them optimum vision: to see, and make out, what he thought he saw, way off in the distance, where the land rose a little to a low ridge of rocks, rather curiously shaped, like teeth, *there*. A horseman, riding his mount without hurry along that ridge, picking his way. An Arab, no doubt, in flowing robe and headcloth, one man, alone. There could be no question of what he was doing out there, unless he chose to ride in, and that was watching the camp. Visitors they had, from time to time, of course, tribesmen, their families, on foot or on camelback, on their way from one place to another: they were entertained, briefly, as custom demanded, and afterwards seen on their way. This was different, a horseman: if he chose to ride in, all right, there might be some perfectly ordinary explanation; if not . . .

But the rider came no closer. After a time disappeared, in the gathering gloom, over the skyline.

★ ★ ★

The mess: a long narrow room with a small bar at one end, a refectory table of sufficient size the other, easy chairs (government issue) in between; shelves of paperbacks on one wall, a few newspapers and magazines scattered about on low tables; a big transistor-radio on a long sideboard. Two a/cs at head height, two vases of plastic greenery and flowers, one on the bar, one on a stand by the door marked 'Kitchen' . . . He got there first, with Jones, who acted as barman and had the keys, crossed the room immediately to the kitchen and opened the door: found Nizam the cook at work. Told him that he might have to hold supper for a while that evening: there was a meeting which could take some time —
Then got a beer from Jones at

47

the bar and settled down in an armchair to wait. The Australian was a tough unapproachable character of few words, in his late forties, a geophysical agronomist (whatever that might be) and there was no need to make conversation. Andersen sipped his beer, leafed through a magazine, running over in his mind the notes he had made — on a folded sheet of paper now in the back pocket of his slacks — of what he was going to say, when the time came; and, very occasionally, glanced either at the watch on his wrist or the radio across the room. 7.30: the national news, in Arabic, from the capital: as day followed day it became increasingly important that they listen, he felt, and keep abreast of events, if any, as they were reported. It was now 7.16.

Maria Sherman, Colette Blofield, the next to arrive, inseparable, as always: both small, grey, dumpy, both a lot of fun when their minds weren't on higher things. He rose, greeted them, and they grinned back at him, eyes twinkling behind what looked to be identical National Health specs. But they were in the middle of an argument, something to do with lasers, and took their sherries over to the dining-table where they could continue it in peace. He did not sit down again; went across to the bar for another beer. Jones had a set of dice on the bartop and rolled him a pair of Kings without saying anything. He rolled two, got another King, so Jones paid —

Stewart-Smith and Hoffmann together: he heard them mount the steps outside, both big men: one an international rugby-footballer decades ago, the other a bearded bear of a man who had gone through hell as a teenager during the war. Both family men and homesick, their quarters full of photos, they were both in this country to work, and did little else. He made way for them at the bar and Stewart-Smith, who didn't drink, had a squash, while Hoffmann had his usual four fingers of cognac which could last him all evening or no time at all.

Finally Peter, and with him Lina Mash'al. She was beautiful, in her narrow-eyed slinky sort of way, dressed simply if provocatively in a sleeveless black blouse, short belted skirt, and heeled sandals, with a little gold at wrist and ears; looked more youthful than she was with her unruly hair and deep tan. That Peter was besotted with her, and a little embarrassed by the fact, had recently become increasingly obvious. Another tall man, their 'leader', raw-boned, prematurely grey (for he was not much more than forty), he looked successful, clever, able, and all of those he undoubtedly was. He escorted the girl to the bar, his hand at her elbow, smiling around and saying hullo to everyone present, and Jones gave them the beers they asked for, pouring from cans with either hand into tall glasses.

Too conscious of her close beside him, Andersen moved away. Looked at his watch again and then went over to the sideboard to collect the radio; put it down on a low table in the centre of the room. Sat down in an armchair, leaning forward, glass in hand, ready to switch on when the time came: one touch of a button needed, that was all, the set already tuned to the correct wavelength. The time 7.28. He looked up, around the room, and caught peoples' eyes. Murmuring together they came, sat down with him, Peter — Elyane Mash'al at his side — opposite him, both watching him, the girl now with a smoking cigarette dangling from the fingers of one hand.

He switched on: static, interference, as usual this side of the mountains; then silence. Silence? A music programme, usually, at this hour, before the news. But silence, continuing silence. Then voices, Arabic, cutting in, peremptory, cut off, indistinct —

"What the hell — ?" Peter began.

"Quiet!" he snapped. "Lina!"

The girl sat forward quickly, listening

intently with him.

More static, more voices, what they said incomprehensible, followed by silence again. He looked at the girl, but she shook her head, frowning; at his watch again: 7.30 now, just gone. Still silence. Then, without warning, the National Anthem, in the form of a slow march, quite clear, and its meaning, surely, unmistakable. Surely, yes . . .

"The Sultan is dead," he said quietly, looking round at the faces watching him. "That has to be it."

No one spoke, people moved in their chairs, sat back, listening to the slow dirge as, intricately, sombrely, it rolled on towards its conclusion. Over Peter's shoulder he saw the kitchen door open and the two Sri Lankans, Nizam and Shams, come in. In their white khansus and cummerbunds they stood in the doorway, waiting, like everyone else. After the National Anthem came the announcement, made by the familiar voice of Abdullah Wahedi, the station's top voice —

'In the name of God, the Compassionate, the Merciful, I bring you tidings of great sorrow. At 6.30 this evening, at his palace at Ras al Ain, His Majesty the Sultan, Sheikh Hamad bin Salim al Sa'adi, passed away. May God rest his soul. Allahu Akbar. At 7.10 local time this evening the medical team attending his Majesty's bedside issued the following bulletin, which I now read in full . . . '

Tempted to switch the set off there and then, Andersen held his hand. Listening on: for further news, if any yet, any developments. His eyes on the girl, who listened with him, her concentration total, eyes down. Apart from the radio no other sound in the room but the hissing breath of the a/cs. But there was nothing more, once the medical bulletin had run its course: only silence once again, interrupted by spitting static. After waiting a minute, two, he reached out, stabbed down with his forefinger and ended it. Said, to Peter,

"The next step is the Embassy, I think."

Peter nodded. "At eight." It was now 7.44.

They all moved restlessly and got to their feet, gathered together round the bar, where Jones began repriming peoples' glasses. Not much talk between them, very little to say and nothing that anyone knew of (of direct relevance to themselves) had actually happened, yet: the Sultan, a good old man and well-loved, had passed on, as expected, that was all. Everyone aware, though, that the situation was now changed, fluid, and the next twenty-four hours probably crucial.

Quietly Andersen confirmed the news to the two Sri Lankans, who spoke little Arabic but weren't fools, telling them that from now on he would keep them abreast of events, as they occurred, they could count on it. Keeping their thoughts to themselves the two men thanked him, salaamed, and returned to work. He then went to the outside door, opened it, and went down the steps, to the Persians and their overseer, Lukman, who had already come across from their trailer and were bunched together, in the full glare of the overhead lights, waiting. Bearded faces turned to him, dark eyes gleaming, hands in pockets or cupping cigarettes, they murmured greetings and then stood silent. Behind him he heard someone else come down the steps from the mess tojoin him: Peter. Using Lukman sometimes to interpret for him he reassured the men that nothing was changed, for the time being, so let them return to their quarters and have their evening meal. In ten minutes time the Ra'is, Peter, would radio the capital and if, after that, there were things to be done, he would let them know. His voice calming, evenly pitched, for these were a volatile people, and the impression he sought to give was one of complete confidence, of plans already thought out and ready to be implemented — for *their* protection as much as that of anyone else, if the need arose.

They heard him out, muttered a little among themselves, shrugged their shoulders and, after a time, nodded agreement. Began trailing off again, back whence they had come. A sudden outburst of harsh laughter among them jarring the night at one point, that was all: some joke, probably crude, that appealed.

To Peter, he said, "Let's go. Call up the Embassy on the dot, yes?"

"I'll get the others," Peter said.

They came down the steps of the mess trailer, some with glasses still in hand, only Jones staying behind. Made for the kabin next to it, Peter's quarters and the radio-shack at one end. He mounted the steps to the door directly behind Elyane Mash'al, and knew that *now* she was as conscious of him as he was of her; without it meaning so much to her, doubtless, but nevertheless. A small beginning that almost certainly led nowhere. At the top of the steps, in Peter's 'office', she waited for him, a little apart from the others, letting them go on ahead. Said, "You'll have your meeting, after this?"

He nodded. "See what the Embassy have to say, first, but even if they say nothing, *still*, we get organised. Tonight."

"You think it may be that urgent?"

"It may be." And he added, "I don't want to die, just yet, do you? Not if there's anything we can do to prevent it."

She was studying his face: half with him, half not, he could see that. But then nodded and said finally, "All right."

He reached out and gripped her arm, briefly, the bare lightly-muscled flesh — to thank her, reassure her — before turning away, leaving her to follow.

The radio-shack a tiny functional room, just big enough for all of them to squeeze into: a worktable, two upright chairs, a calendar on the wall under the a/c, the big Toshiba on its wide custom-built stand under the curtained window. Beside it a stabiliser and a spaghetti maze of wiring, to a power-point, to the antennae on the roof. Peter had already switched on, stood beside the set now, receiver in hand, waiting for everything to warm up. Over peoples' shoulders, Andersen could see his face, half-turned away, grimacing in concentration, as he sought about for pencil and notepad and made space for them on the surface before him. Silence in the little room, as though everyone was holding his or her breath: Andersen conscious of Lina Mash'al just behind him, the perfume she was wearing, and all at once she put her hand on his shoulder, and kept it there, supporting herself in the confined space. He didn't look round, though it took an effort not to do so.

Peter depressed his call-button. Began, "Britam, this is Ayoun. Ayoun calling Britam. Britam, do you read me, over?"

No reply. Static only.

Again, "Britam! Britam, this is

Ayoun. Are you reading me, over?"

Nothing. Peter looked round, eyebrows raised. Tried again. And again. Demanding, cajoling. Nothing, not a word, from anywhere. It became obvious that, unless there was something wrong with the set (which was unlikely), either there was no operator on duty the other end, for the time being, or — something worse had happened. After a final try, again unsuccessful, Peter switched off. Turned and said quietly, "They're probably very busy. We'll call them again in half an hour." He sought Anderson's eyes across the room, and smiled crookedly. Said, "Jack, if you're ready, we should perhaps have that meeting of yours, straight away."

3

THEY had their meeting, ate quickly, tried to contact the Embassy again, with no greater success than before. Listened to the News on the BBC World Service at nine, which told them nothing, did not even report the Sultan's death — and after that went to work. Peter on stand-by in the radio-shack, Colette Blofield in the mess with the big transistor tuned to London beside her; the rest getting on with it. Getting vehicles, fuel, and other vital stores, to safety inside the ring of trailers; rigging lights, which would burn all night, along the line of the big cable which brought power into camp from the generators, so that, with luck, the watchmen to be stationed out there would run no risk of being taken by surprise. The best they could do, this, until the morning when, it had been decided, they would move the generators themselves, but that was a major task and they hoped against hope that in the event it might not be necessary, that they would get news, good news of some sort, overnight.

Their armoury consisted of two rook-rifles, that was all, .256 Husqvarnas and twenty-five rounds for each. They were small, light, but still with considerable stopping-power, and had been provided by Andersen from Embassy Stores a month and more ago, with the thought of gazelle in mind, for the pot, among other things. But until this day no one had used them, they had all been too busy; apart from that, besides himself, only Stewart-Smith knew one end of a long gun from the other; he and, surprisingly, Elyane Mash'al, or so, at the meeting, she had said . . .

9.30, the night starlit and a little chill, and after being told to get lost by Jones, in charge of moving vehicles and gas — after seeing that Hoffmann had everything he needed to set out his lights — he took his two riflemen outside the ring, beyond the lab, where they were not so much in public view, to see if the two of them really knew what they were about, or not. Stewart-Smith in a donkey-jacket now, like himself; Elyane changed into windcheater and jeans. He gave them a weapon each, broke open a box of shells and told them to load. Stewart-Smith taking his time: he weighed the rifle in his hands, looked it over closely, holding it up to the lights; then broke out the magazine confidently enough and began filling it, taking three rounds from the box Andersen held out to him. No problem — but Elyane a revelation, and he felt the hair prickling along the back of his neck as he watched her. She handled the weapon as if it were her own, loaded three rounds into the magazine with quick dexterous movements of fingers and hand, banged the bolt home, and then threw the rifle to her shoulder, sighting along the barrel into the night.

Finally thumbed down the safety-catch, and handed the weapon back to him. Said, with a broad grin, "That surprised you, didn't it?"

He nodded, smiling a little in return, but saved his questions for another time. Asked seriously, "Could you kill with it?"

"If I was threatened, yes, or those whom I loved."

He busied himself unloading both guns. When that was done, looked up at her again. She stood legs apart, hands in pockets, facing him, her eyes expressionless. "Why don't you go in and get some sleep?" he suggested. "Mark and I can stand watch. We'll call you if we need you."

"No."

"Hell, *yes*," he said. "Two on at a time ought to be enough."

★ ★ ★

She rejoined him again at eleven, saying she couldn't sleep anyway. Bringing news, which was no news, that Peter was still unable to get through to the Embassy; that he had tried to call up Abu Dhabi, Sharjah, the army base at Jibra, all usually within range, but had found no one to talk to them; that the air-waves seemed to be carrying a fair amount of traffic but nearly all of it in code. She also reported that the BBC were putting out news now of the Sultan's death, so Colette said, but little more than that: no advice yet to expats in the country or anything of that kind. From all of which you could deduce both good and bad, as you felt inclined, and that was pointless, so Peter had sent Colette to bed and gone to kip down for an hour or two himself.

They set out along the line of lights towards the generators, where Stewart-Smith was. From under the roof of corrugated iron he came out to meet them, rifle at the trail, thumbing the baseball cap he was wearing to the back of his head. Quickly she told him her news, such as it was, and he shrugged, nodded, and wondered if what they were doing was really necessary.

"I think so," Andersen said. "Yes." He had said nothing, to any of them, of the sight of that horseman, earlier, in the desert, and didn't propose to now. Nevertheless that man, and what he had probably been doing, gave him no cause at all for thinking of diminishing their vigilance at this stage. The reverse, with the dog-watches of the night yet to come. Still, it didn't need all three of them. So, to Stewart-Smith he said, "You go on in now, until say one. Lina and I can look after things until then."

"Why not," Stewart-Smith said, gave the girl his weapon and ammo and took off, yawning and blowing on his hands, back to camp.

They walked together, out into the desert a little way, and sat down on the sand, a yard or so apart, the girl keeping an eye on the generators and the line of lights, he facing the other way, the darkness of the night. The talk between them unforced, quiet, and as the spirit moved.

"You're not tired?" he asked.

"I was, but I'm not now. You?"

"I'll sleep all day tomorrow. Maybe. I hope." He got out cigarettes, lit two, and passed her one. Said seriously, "How *did* you learn to handle a rifle, anyway?"

"Simple, really," she said. "I'm Lebanese. You know?"

"I know."

"So one day I thought I'd go back and work in my country, if I get the chance. The Lebanon is an archaeologist's dream and hardly touched. But it's a country with problems, is it not? Problems, always."

"So it seemed a good idea to be prepared?"

"Right. I joined a rifle-club, found I had a good eye, and then got really interested." She turned her head. "You? You were in the Services, I think."

66

"Yes, that's how I started, after college."

"What branch? Infantry, tanks, what?"

"I was in the SAS," he said. No inflection in his voice.

"Were you, indeed?" She was really watching him now, eyebrows raised. Asked, "Why did you come out?"

"I was wounded, in Malaya, not badly but badly enough. You have to be a hundred percent, in that game."

"You regret, having to quit?"

"Oh yes," he said. Then, "Does that surprise you?"

She thought about it. Then, as though she had decided to be as honest as she could be, said thoughtfully, "It's a world I know nothing about, that my world has no time for and has always denigrated. In that I have always paid lip-service to conventional 'wisdom', as I found it. But a part of me *is* Lebanese, as I said, and that part understands the SAS all right and knows why they are needed. Is more than grateful that they exist."

He said nothing for a time after that. Then, carefully, not looking at her, "I would like very much, to know you better. If this all sorts itself out, and we're still here, maybe I can show you parts of this country that I love which you may not have been to. If you have the time?"

"I'd like that," she said, without hesitation. "And time can always be made."

* * *

He came a long time after midnight, when there was no moon: a wiry dark-skinned youth, near-naked, with a knife between his teeth. He knew just what he was going to do and did it with ruthless efficiency.

First he waited, out in the dark, near the generators. Studied the watchman there, seated in a deckchair under one corner of the corrugated-iron roof, his rifle between his knees: half-asleep and facing left. A big man, heavy-shouldered, wearing a baseball cap. Already knew where the other watchman was: half-way down the line of lights supported on orange-boxes, between generators and kabins, and that one sitting cross-legged on the ground: staring about him from time to time, but not often . . . So picked his time, just after the second watchman had straightened his back for a few moments, as he was getting a cigarette alight. Muttered a quick prayer to God, and then went in, grabbed the big man's head from behind and knifed him across the throat, cutting deep and his own breath hissing between his teeth, but such small sounds as were made of no consequence in the racket the generators were putting out.

Blood, gouts of it, and he lugged the chair the man was sitting in round a little, so that the body within it might not be so easily seen, holding the body still as he did so, and then letting it slump down, the head loose on the shoulder. Took the rifle and ran off with it then, back into the night. Ten seconds, that's all it had taken him, the whole thing. And the second watchman hadn't moved. God be praised. Still, to waste no time, now.

He left the rifle where he could find it again, then circled the camp, in the night. Went in at a crouching run between the raised kabins, straight to the three vehicles and the drums of fuel beside them. Took cover in the shadow cast by the big Nissan, let his breathing quieten while he looked round. Dark, all the kabins, except one, its door open and a man moving about inside: the kabin with the radio-antennae above it in one corner . . . Keeping an eye on that kabin from time to time he set to work: he knew vehicles, especially desert-vehicles, had driven and roughly maintained a battered Toyota for years. So knew where to strike without making a sound. Getting under each one in turn and, by feel, reaching up, slashing fanbelts and rubber tubing, ripping out wiring: bloodying his knuckles, tearing his nails, but never mind, his whole self in a state of exhilaration at the destruction he was causing — and if the alarm were to be given, well, so be it, he was ready to die, and gladly, doing what he had come to do. But no alarm was raised, not while he was under any of the vehicles, and when he had done enough he escaped the way he had come.

One more thing. He returned to the generators, still thudding away under their light-ringed shelter. The second watchman had moved, was on his feet, relieving himself a little way away from the path of lights leading to them: what would he do after that? If he came over to the generators, to contact the man who had been on watch there, he, Ashraf, would kill him. But he did not come, and when he had finished relieving himself, settled down again by the line of lights, his rifle at his side.

One of the generators suddenly shut itself down as they were designed to do from time to time: not so much output needed during the hours of darkness. Ideal, and he went to that one first, ignoring the body of the man he had killed in its chair not six feet from him. Reached up and using his hands and a rag unscrewed the big 'cap' above the silent pistons, threw it behind him into the night. Then ferried desert sand in an empty can he found, three times, and poured it into the engine. Went from the back-up generator to the one in action, getting everything ready this time before making his move: cap off, a canful of sand ready to use. Then, after a last look round, emptied it in. Turned and ran, teeth gritted, nursing one hand which had got badly burnt.

A second or two only, then a shattering grinding of gears, the generator blew up, and darkness fell.

4

THEY buried Stewart-Smith in the sand beside the trail to 'Ayoun 1' shortly after first light, four of the remaining men taking it in turns to dig while one kept watch. Then all gathered while Hoffmann read a prayer over the pile of stones under which the body lay. After that everyone returned to camp where the Sri Lankans, working on a primus, had hot coffee and a bit of breakfast prepared. Their mood grim, and Maria Sherman tearful.

Their situation was now critical. They had water, food, for a fortnight, but no transport, power, or lighting, other than two hurricane lanterns and a few torches; they had one rifle and fifty rounds. It was possible, Jones said, that he *might* be able to get one of the four-wheel-drive vehicles to run, in time, but they shouldn't bank on it: he was not that sort of mechanic and the spares available on site were meagre, a fanbelt or two, new sets of points, not much else: nothing to make him at all confident that he could deal with the real destruction that their intruder had achieved. And even if he did succeed, where were they to go? The morning news on the BBC had at last a certain amount of information to give them, all of it terrifying: telling of chaos, probable civil war, in the capital; of the 'bombing' of the British Embassy, among others, not an hour after the old Sultan's death; of tribal warfare raising its ugly head elsewhere: all this reported by fugitives reaching Abu Dhabi by road during the night. Via the BBC the Foreign Office advised all British residents to lie low, *stay put*, keep their heads down, for the time being, to do nothing else. All very well, but in their case other factors were involved, local ones, as the events of the night had proved, and they might be under threat of attack at any moment.

Andersen put Lina, with the rifle, on the roof of the mess, to keep watch all round on the surrounding desert and bergs, while the rest of them talked below, with the exception of Maria who had gone to bed. Five of them round the refectory table, the two Sri Lankans sitting uneasily on bar-stools across the room, all windows and doors open to give them light and air. Not hot, for an hour or two yet, but later these kabins would be almost unlivable in. One thing, for better or worse, they did not have to worry about: the Persians and their overseer, who had run off, God knew where, and whether in panic or by design, during the hours of darkness. Probably *before* their intruder had made his move, Andersen suspected.

That he blamed himself, at least partly, for Stewart-Smith's death went without saying: he looked drawn, very weary, as he put to the others the possibilities, as he saw them, and

75

took their comments and suggestions in return. To go, or not to go, to move or not to move, those were the questions.

"I'll start," Jones said, "on the Nissan. It's in a hell of a mess but perhaps not so badly off as the other two. I'll need people's help."

"If even one vehicle can be repaired," Peter said. "It surely improves our options enormously — "

"If they give us time," Andersen said.

"*Who*, Goddammit? Why should they want to finish us?" Peter again, avoiding the use of the word 'kill'. "What have they got against us?"

"I don't know," Andersen said. "And I don't know who 'they' are, though I might hazard a guess. Maybe it's simply a matter of plunder, an eye on the main chance — "

"It's more than that," Hoffmann said quietly.

Andersen nodded. "I think so too."

"If it *is* only plunder," Peter said,

"let us give them whatever they want. They can have it, and welcome, in exchange for our lives."

"I can go out there and try to contact them," Andersen said. "I can go to Kamil, if necessary. I doubt that it will do any good, but I can try it."

"On foot?"

"It's not so far. But while I'm away," he looked round, "you *do not stay here*. Understood? These kabins, this place, it's a death-trap. You move to those bergs out there, find a suitable spot near the top which you have some chance of defending and from which you can keep watch. You only come down to these kabins in daylight and when you see it's safe to do so."

"No good," Peter said suddenly. "I can't permit it, you going out to contact those people, by yourself. If you're right about their intentions they will only kill you, or take you hostage."

"Can you think of anything better?" Andersen asked.

"No, I can't. But at least wait until

Jones here has had a go at the Nissan. Who knows, we may be able to use it, after all."

It made sense, and there the matter was left, for the time being.

★ ★ ★

The morning wore on, and the heat mounted. While Lina tried to get some sleep, he kept watch from the roof of the mess, seated on a camp-stool and with a golf-umbrella to protect him a little from the sun, the rifle in his hands. From his eyrie he had a good view, in some directions for miles and miles over sand and low scrubland, but from those directions it was unlikely that any threat to them might come. Three locations, all within half a mile of camp, provided the possibility of far greater and immediate danger: the ridge, to the south, where he had seen his horseman the evening before; the belt of trees, beyond the Ayoun mounds, this side of the wadi; and the bergs, to the east and quite close, from the cover of whose crests a marksman could pick them off without difficulty — all it needed was a good eye and a good gun. He never let his eyes stray far from those crests for very long. But so far that morning had seen nothing.

Below him, in the ring of trailers, Jones, Hoffmann, Peter and the three vehicles: bonnets laid back; Jones painstakingly working on the guts of the Nissan, works-manual open on a stool at his side, replacing damaged parts with spares, if he had them, improvising others, to the best of his ability — tubing, wiring — with bits and pieces taken from the Pajero and the LR: all three men stripped to the waist, floppy hats on their heads, their hands, their arms blackened with oil, their bodies shiny with sweat. To one side the rusting cylinders, tubing, mask of the welding equipment which Jones was using from time to time. By midday, the Australian said, he would have a pretty clear idea whether the thing was really on, or not.

At five to eleven he heard Colette Blofield come to the door of the mess-kabin below him and call out the time: a BBC broadcast due on the hour and detailed instructions to Brits still left in the country expected. Below him the three men straightened up from whatever they were doing, began cleaning themselves up a bit before going inside; from two trailers away Lina Mash'al came down the steps of the girls' kabin and turned to look up at him, shading her eyes with her hand. He stood up and prepared to hand over to her again. She came across and began mounting the ladder to the mess roof. He took a very careful final look round, but still nothing, no one to be seen, out there: the crests, still nothing.

She wore trousers, a check shirt, its tails tied under her breasts, leaving her midriff bare, and for the first time ever, as he reached out the rifle to her, he couldn't quite face her, and had to look away. Her face puffy from lack of sleep and great heat, dark rings under her eyes, her physical 'presence' yet almost tangible, calling to him as, surely to God, it would call to many men. Many men, some of whom, given the chance, would use her without mercy and when they had done with her throw her away. For all her guts and self-confidence, and perhaps at least partly because of those attributes, they would enjoy breaking her. Aware now, as if his eyes were suddenly opened, of what might happen to her, if all this — this of their situation — did go really wrong. More wrong than it already had. Death, for her, not the only possibility, in a country such as this: a worse fate, for a woman of her pride and accomplishments, not so difficult to imagine. Aware also that she herself understood pretty well what her prospects might be, if, but asked no favours: kept her fears well-hidden while getting on with whatever there was to be done. So, Goddammit, let him try to ensure that she was never 'taken', that above all; let him bear that in mind, all the time, from now on.

"Can I borrow your sunglasses," she said. "I've left mine behind. I'm still half-asleep, really."

"Of course." He passed them to her and she put them on. "Watch those crests over there, those especially," he said, pointing. "Bang on the roof, hard, if you see anything moving."

"I will."

* * *

The news was not good. Street fighting in the capital, elements of the army loyal to the old regime fighting other elements, the edifice of the state fragmenting on tribal lines; in the coastal towns total breakdown of law and order; of events in the interior nothing known. The capital's radio putting out order of the day after order of the day, apparently in the hands of Marxist stroke Fundamentalist factions under the leadership of the old Sultan's nephew, Sheikh Suhaim . . . After the news, the FO's advice and instructions, and they listened to them, the radio on the dining-table in their midst, Colette with a pad of paper before her and ballpoint pen in hand, taking notes —

The Swedish Embassy coordinating evacuation, which was to take place, commencing 1800 hours that day, by sea: a Royal Navy frigate, the *Alcyone*, would be off the coast at Ras Bora beach ten miles from the capital by that time and with it one or more merchant ships now making for the scene. All holders of British passports strongly advised to get out of the country: to meet at, and get themselves to, the Cable and Wireless Compound at Niba, six miles inland from the capital, and wait there; then in convoy, with nationals of other countries and under Red Cross auspices, make their way to the coast at times to be arranged. That was all. Instructions repeated a second time, but that was all.

When the broadcast was over, Peter looked round. Said quietly, "All right, that's it. You all heard, and that's what we'll do." He corrected himself — "try to do." His eyes singling out Jones. "All we need is one vehicle in working order." He turned away, shrugged, and finished sadly, "Jesus, what a godawful mess."

Andersen very nearly spoke up then, gave them the alternative that he knew of and they did not, but held his peace. Time enough for that alternative, later, if Jones did not succeed. Time enough because, including the two Sri Lankans, there were nine people at Ayoun and, realistically, that alternative had no chance of success with so many, no chance at all.

5

HE made up his mind, what he personally would do, shortly after two o'clock, after a weary Jones had announced that, despite his worst fears, the Nissan did now run. Held together with string and insulation tape she might be, her innards a hotchpotch of borrowed tubing and improvised wiring, she was a going concern once more and, given luck, would get them to the capital. Apart from Andersen, on watch, they all stood around while Jones started her up, ran her back and forth a few times within the confines of the ring of kabins and then switched off; got down to their congratulations and heartfelt thanks . . . Immediately, Peter called another meeting but they did not go inside, the interior of the kabins being now untenable in the intense heat, but squatted or settled down in the narrow strip of shade either side of the mess steps. There Andersen joined them, came to stand behind Elyane Mash'al — seated, her arms clasped about her knees — leaving his watch for however long it took, the rifle in the crook of his elbow.

The three men who had been working on the vehicle, particularly Jones, were exhausted, Peter said, and anyway by now it was too hot, and they weren't ready, to think of travelling straight away. So let everyone rest for a few hours as best they could, with a view to making a start around five. If they did that, then they could hope to make it as far as the main road, forty miles distant, by dusk, in the vicinity of which they would spend the night. Then, starting in the early hours of the following morning, make a run for the capital. Given good fortune, and providing nothing and no one prevented them, they should then reach Niba, the Cable and Wireless complex there, around four in the afternoon, not a bad time to arrive, perhaps, in the hope of going straight on and through to Ras Bora that day.

No comment. Everyone agreed. What Peter suggested made sense and gave them renewed cause for hope. Made sense, so long as you did not allow your mind to dwell on the possibility of people waiting for you, just waiting, out in the desert, not far away perhaps or at any rate somewhere between camp and main road, who were there for one reason only: to shoot you down and take all you had. If you didn't think too much about that, or the dangers to be faced during the course of two hundred and fifty miles of hard driving the next day, across country, through villages and towns in the grip, almost certainly, of civil war . . .

There would be very little room to spare in the Nissan, Peter went on, in fact they would be crammed in like sardines in a can. But still they must have food — for at least three days — iron rations, drinking water: Maria and Colette, with the Sri Lankans, would please attend to that.

The two women said they would.

They must have petrol and oil, spare cans, as many as could be fitted in: Jones, Hoffmann, after resting, would please work out a seating-plan, bearing that in mind, and then get the additional fuel loaded.

The two men mentioned nodded thoughtfully.

They must have blankets, one each — they could sit on them — they must have torches, matches to make a fire, toilet paper, water-purification tablets; he, Peter, with Lina's help, would personally see to those things plus anything else that might occur to anyone as being of vital necessity. What they could not do, he was very sorry, was bring anything with them either of a personal nature (other than the clothes they stood up in) or, of greater concern to them all, perhaps, anything connected with their work.

He regretted it as much as they, but there just wasn't going to be enough room, and if once he started making exceptions to that rule, there was likely to be no end to it. One day, he consoled them, and quite soon, maybe, they could well be returning to this site and hopefully, before then, not too much of what they had achieved, and found there, would have been ruined, vandalised, or stolen . . . He said no more. Looked round, inviting their comments, further suggestions, if any.

But they had none, not at any rate for the time being. Sat waiting, in silence, for someone to make a move.

Finally Peter turned his head and looked up at Andersen. Said, "Jack, you've got to get some rest too, for God's sake. You were up all night."

"I'll manage," Andersen said, shaking his head. "I'll be OK." With the muzzle of the rifle, as though by accident, he made a small movement, touching Lina Mash'al in the small of her back, so that she also looked round, and up at him. Choosing his words with great care, he said what he had come to say, then, quite quietly. "When you leave at five, I'll not be going with you. Now, please!" — peremptorily, to silence murmurs of surprise and any questioning — "I know what I'm doing, and I've thought the thing through. There is another way out of this country, that I know of, but it is not one that a group, such as you are, can take. You would have no chance, I promise you, or I'd tell you of it — "

"Not good enough!" Peter snapped, staring at him.

"It has to be," Andersen said evenly, and turned away.

★ ★ ★

Four o'clock in the afternoon, an hour before departure, and a little cooler now. He had asked her to come with him when he went up to the crests of the bergs near camp, to take a last look round. The two of them stood side by side on one of the highest points, from which they had a superb view in every direction, of the desert, and the wadi, and the trail leading off across the sand to Kamil and the main road. They had a pair of field-glasses with them and passed them from one to the other, but there was nothing to be seen out there, nothing moved, either in the vicinity of camp or in the distance.

"Perhaps they've gone?" she said, after a time.

"They may have," he agreed.

"But you don't think so?"

"No." He sat down on a rock and looked up at her, rifle across his knees. Said only, "They're not the kind of people, who go."

She said nothing. Then, after a moment, "We have to try it."

"The others, *they* have to try it. Not you."

"Meaning?"

"You come with me." And, at her look, "If you like, come with me."

"Why?"

"You know why."

"Do I?" she asked. Then, coldly, with a shake of her head, "So tell me, what you're offering. What is it you're going to do anyway?"

Suddenly he laughed, taking her by surprise and rivetting her attention upon him whether she liked it or not. "What I propose is probably madness," he said. "Anyway, that's what you may think. I'm going to walk, that way" — he pointed, to the north — "head for the mountains, cross them, and make for a place on the coast called Ras Abu Khim — "

"You *are* crazy," she said. Deliberately she half-turned from him. "What d'you mean, 'walk'? It's seventy miles or more, to the mountains. There's no water — "

"I'll only have to walk some of the way, I hope," he said. "And as for water, you're wrong. There is water, if you know where to look for it. Also, there are villages."

"All right, so there's water, and

villages. There's a thousand other things."

"True." He nodded, serious again. Went on, "I don't minimise the dangers, not one bit, but that way, I believe, there's *some* chance, and I want to live." He stared at her. "I'm damn well determined to live, in fact, if I can."

"I don't understand, I really don't," she said. Moved away, a few steps, before swinging round to face him again. Said, after a moment, "You can't have the rifle, you know, we'll need the rifle, with *us*."

"I don't want the bloody rifle," he said. "I don't intend to *fight* my way through. I have a knife, a good one, that's all I need."

She had nothing more to say, for the time being, so held her peace. Knew only that this man was in deadly earnest and meant to do exactly what he said, for reasons which to him seemed sufficient. Knew also that he had the courage, very probably, and the will, not to mention the depth of experience required, to give him at least some chance of success. Knew finally that she had never before come across anyone even remotely like him. The fact remained that what he proposed, for himself, and now *for her*, appeared foolhardy to the point of utter recklessness, when there remained, did there not, the other way? For all the risks and uncertainties involved in *that*, it was still so much quicker, so much easier, provided it worked.

"You *want* to take off on your own, don't you?" she asked curiously. "That's really what all this is about, isn't it?"

"Yes," he admitted, watching her intently again. Went on quietly, "Would I be wrong in thinking that the idea has a certain appeal for you, also?"

"I *cannot* go with you," she said flatly. Thinking of Peter now, to whom she owed a great deal and from whom she had taken much — and of a life, her own, lived in a particular way, with goals that for some years past had seemed attainable — "I couldn't cope. I'd get in your way."

"No, I don't think so." He shook his head and stood up. "The very reverse, in fact. You really begin to *care*, when you're not alone." He glanced at her, concluding, "That probably sounds selfish."

"Honest, anyway," she said. And shrugged.

Again his eyes roved over the desert, taking in both the camp itself and its surroundings, then probing further out, into the far distance. Still nothing to be seen, anywhere. But there were gullies, depressions, out there in the desert, many folds in the terrain in which men and vehicles could lie up and remain invisible, biding their time, he knew it: the desert here much like the desert anywhere else. Eventually he said, "If you go with the others, you won't get five miles in all probability."

"And if I come with you?"

"You may die, but not today, I

hope." And with that he turned away, to start down again. Saying, over his shoulder, "I'm going now, to get a few things together. I want to be on my way before the others take off. If you're coming with me, get what you need together in one bag, something that you can carry without too much difficulty, and I'll see you by the mess in half an hour. Don't forget water and a blanket." He raised a hand, paused as if to say more, but then was on his way, down the rock-strewn slope of the berg.

★ ★ ★

When they arrived back within the ring of kabins, he went straight to Peter who, with Hoffmann and Nizam, was loading up the Nissan, and handed over the rifle; then headed for his quarters. She watched him go, the powerfully-built, essentially enigmatic figure of a man: a man who had so far given her nothing, but promised — what? Danger, desperate suffering, very probably, but also unforgettable experience — if they came through it — life, shared happiness, unique achievement, it was all there, maybe, there for the taking, if she went with him. She was tempted, and knew it: wary of him still, nowhere near convinced, but also attracted now both physically and emotionally: wanted to be part of his undertaking, and contribute to it whatever strength *she* had. But turned away immediately, to Peter, and asked what she could do to help.

Find an empty carton, Peter said, then go to his kabin and put into it the things she would find stacked ready on the desk in his office. Bring the carton, when filled, back here to the vehicle.

So she did that, her mind in neutral. Found a carton in the kitchen; then filled it, with the bits and pieces that Peter had collected together: the radio, salt tablets, some basic medical supplies, and the rest. Took it out to the Nissan. Jones with Hoffmann now, Peter on watch on the roof of the lab, Colette and Maria coming down the steps of the store-kabin with folded blankets in their arms. Andersen nowhere to be seen.

She helped the two men rope the three four-gallon cans of fuel, two others of water. Then, because it was a quarter to five and they were nearly ready to go, went off to her kabin to change. To go or not to go with the others; to go with Andersen: the decision to be made now unpostponable, and her mind still refusing to do what she asked of it, work out the pros and cons of the thing, as far as she knew them or could imagine. So she changed, into khaki slacks, bush shirt, taking her time deliberately, seeing little of her surroundings. Fear, of the unknown, and of making a terrible mistake, with her, as it had never been with her, she was quite certain before: a sensation of being trapped and of personal inadequacy, and of being at the mercy of Fate. Fear of death, sudden or lingering, *whichever* way she now chose to turn. She was waiting, she realised, weakly, for something in the nature of a sign —

One there, on the floor of her wardrobe: a rucksack. All at once she noticed it, left lying among plastic bags and pairs of shoes: a blue canvas rucksack with white straps; they had all been issued with one like it before departing the UK months before. Useless things, not needed — not needed, until, perhaps, today. She went over to her wardrobe, knelt down, and got it out. Got to her feet again and stood with it in her hands, utterly still, for a few moments; and then took it over to her bed and began packing things into it. Working with trembling haste for a minute or two — underclothes, a shirt, a sarong, sneakers — before straightening up, savagely angry with herself: to think, think, and think again, coldly, knowing that her life might depend on it, that was all that was required now. A torch, a tooth-brush, tampax: socks, more socks, another pair of lightweight boots, a sweater: enough: room left inside for a canteen of water, a spare canteen, for she could carry another at her belt. Room, in the outside pockets, for some food, which she would get from the kitchen, food of various kinds, and a knife, a spoon: God help them, how could the two of them possibly carry all they might need? Not possible, so take only what was absolutely essential: a blanket, from her bed, that she could sling over one shoulder, a hat, sunglasses, of course.

Hefting her rucksack in one hand, the blanket in the other, she went quickly to the outside door of the kabin, sweat pouring off her now; afraid suddenly that Andersen might already have gone.

But he was still there. Sat on the steps leading up to the mess, in the shade, by himself, a big laden sack on the ground at his feet. The others? They came and went still, some of them, only Colette, Maria and Peter seemed to be ready, waiting by the big jeep.

She took what she had and went across the ring to the mess, looking neither to right nor left. Halted before Andersen and said simply, "I can take two canteens of water, but I haven't any food yet."

He was smiling, watching her, his voice when he spoke very gentle. "You're sure?" he asked. "Truly certain?"

She shook her head. "No, but I'm coming anyway."

"I'm glad. Let's go then." And he got up, turned to mount the steps and go inside.

She was about to follow when Peter called her name, so she turned again and waited for him. The look on his face, as he came over, questioning, unable to believe. "You going with him? Lina — ?"

She held up her hand, halting him in his tracks. Said only, "Yes, I'm going with him. So — goodbye. Take care, *please* take care, all of you. And good luck."

6

AGAIN they were up among the crests of the bergs, but this time had got there by a roundabout route and, once up there, took care to remain hidden from view. Lay now in a small hollow among the rocks, Andersen watching the camp below, the wadi, and the trail leading off across the desert beyond; the girl facing the other way, raising her head from time to time to keep watch on the desert to the south. The time: 5.20.

In the circle of kabins everyone left had at last, apparently, got themselves organised and ready for departure. He had seen them climb one by one into the jeep, front and back; then someone — Hoffmann, surely — got out again to trot over to the stores for some item forgotten: more room in the jeep now, that was a bonus for them; they could

103

fit in a few extra supplies. Then he
heard the sound of the jeep's engine,
the full-throated six-cylinder roar of
power that easily carried to him, and
the jeep turned on the sand (with Jones
driving, doubtless) and made for the
way out, between men's quarters and
stores. He called to the girl and she
crawled over to join him, lay down
at his side. He passed her the field-
glasses, but she didn't use them for
the moment.

Once clear of the kabins the jeep
followed the track to the burial-
mounds, Ayoun One, Two and Three:
Jones taking his time, not pushing the
jeep until he was sure of her, the
people inside getting settled, bracing
their feet where they could, finding
convenient metal to hang on to when
the jeep pitched and rolled on the
uneven ground. Five hundred yards
to the mounds and the trees close
beyond; for a time, among them, the
jeep disappeared from view altogether.
Then, at the wadiside, came to a stop,

104

briefly, while Jones banged her into low-ratio to make the crossing: gravel, pebbles beneath the wheels; it was easy enough to stall and bog down, getting across, it had happened to them before, once or twice.

Not this time, and the Nissan ground its way across without difficulty, climbed the bank amidst low scrub the other side.

"Now," Andersen said quietly, "I wonder which way he'll go. He can head off across the desert, try to slip by them, or stick to the trail, put his foot down and hope for the best."

"Which would you do?" she asked.

"Go for it, I think," he said. "Hope to outrun them, if they're still around. Bad though the trail may be in parts, at least you know it's there and you can drive on it, off it you can never be sure."

But Jones, and Peter, didn't see it that way, so it seemed. Fifty yards the other side of the wadi they saw the big dark green vehicle swing off left onto the sands and then head away, almost at right angles to the trail, in a northwesterly direction: not fast, a steady twenty-five perhaps, as Jones and those in the front seat with him kept close watch on the terrain immediately ahead of them. Twisting, turning, making small detours from time to time, the jeep ploughed on, attached to the dust-cloud of its own making: its course beginning to loop back gradually until it was running approximately parallel to the main trail and may be a half-mile from it. How long they would have continued on that course before swinging back towards the trail again it was impossible to say, because all at once and without the slightest warning they were not alone —

Andersen grunted, pointing, snatching up the glasses and raising them to his eyes. Beside him the girl tensed, and held her breath —

Three jeeps, a little way off the trail, to the left, they had appeared as if by magic out of the ground, and set off now like dark insects of prey across the sand to head off the Nissan. Bedu drivers doubtless, far more expert than Jones at handling their vehicles in trackless conditions, years of it behind them, their vehicles lighter, stripped to the bone, they began inexorably to overhaul their quarry. Jones putting on all the speed he could, aware suddenly of the danger behind him, pouring power into the Nissan's engine, taking risks, hurling his passengers about as the jeep plunged and skidded across the uneven terrain. Useless: he was forced to turn sharply by some obstacle in his path, lost momentum, and the three predators fanned out, two of them swinging wide to take him on either flank. All at once the chase was over and the Nissan stopped: why, it was impossible to tell; perhaps, quite simply, the engine had seized up.

She had the field-glasses now and the tableau of jeeps and men, out there, in clear view. Could not really credit what she was witnessing, bit by bit, as the scenario unfolded; until it happened and she was forced to believe in it. Massacre, out there in the desert.

From the three jeeps six or seven men, all armed with rifles, leaped out. Ringing the stalled Nissan they lay prone, trained their weapons upon Peter and his companions as they got down and showed themselves, hands in the air. Then — at a shouted word of command, perhaps — firing commenced, clearly audible, a ragged volley. Followed by a second volley, as Jones began to run at them, to take them on, and the others threw themselves flat, whether seeking cover or because they were hit it was impossible to say. Jones down, his body splayed out jerking in the dust, one of the women and one of the Sri Lankans up and reeling away, trying to make it back to the Nissan, but both immediately smashed down by rifle-fire to lie spread-eagled with the others.

He grabbed the field-glasses from her

and she dropped her head on her arms, closing her eyes tight, her body still. Remained that way for a few seconds before looking up again. Out in the desert the six Arabs were finishing off what they had begun —

Single shots from hand-guns, as they closed in, circled the Nissan and dealt with the wounded, one by one. Then they swarmed over the big jeep and took from it a few things they wanted: blankets, the tool-box, two four-gallon containers, probably of petrol. Nondescript men and youths, in belted thobes, rifles still in hand, folds of their headgear wrapped round mouths and throat so that only their eyes were visible. When they had finished with the Nissan, three of them detached themselves from the others to go and bring up their jeeps, into the backs of which and working in pairs they threw the bodies. Then climbed aboard and headed away across the desert towards the trail.

He watched them a few moments

longer, until the three vehicles reached the trail and turned onto it, turned to head in the direction of the campsite. Then grabbed her arm and moved back quickly from the skyline, taking her with him. Said sharply, "Come on, let's get out of here."

★ ★ ★

It was nearly dark and they were marching, across the desert, the south wind, the evening wind, in their faces.

"What will they do, back there?" she asked, her voice low. She had been silent for some time, and he hadn't known what to say to her.

"They were under orders, I think," he said. "Otherwise they'd surely have stripped the bodies and left them where they lay. But they expected all of us to fall into their trap, and we didn't."

"So they'll come after us, tonight?"

"Unlikely," he said. "They'll search the camp first and when they don't find us they'll use the light that's left to look for our tracks in the other direction. That's the way we ought to be heading."

"Where *are* we going?"

"Budeiya," he said. "You've been there, if I remember?"

More than a month ago, yes, she did indeed remember: she, Peter and Stewart-Smith had visited Budeiya to have a look round and see if the place held any interest for them: an early-Islamic village, finally abandoned fifty or more years ago, in the desert. Remote, beautiful, rather eerie, it was only ten miles from Ayoun, yet it had taken them all of two hours to get there by Land Rover over some very rough and stony terrain, quite trackless. Not a bad place to head for in the first instance, she suspected, no, not a bad place at all: Budeiya with its leaning walls, sunken 'gardens' and sloping drifts of sand. As good a place as any in which to seek refuge.

They walked on, and night fell. Starlight and the vast bowl of the night sky above them, the air quite cool: Andersen with his sack over one shoulder or the other; herself hitching the straps of the rucksack on her back from time to time to ease the chafing and growing discomfort. Never mind, her body felt strong and capable of keeping going for as long as it had to; and they could see their way, most of the time, much better than she had expected, without using lights. He especially: the desert by night, its shadows and pitfalls no great problem to him, obviously, he had done this sort of thing before, many times probably, and gave her his hand whenever the going became at all difficult, until her confidence grew. Confidence, also a resurgence of hope, a feeling of deliverance (and closeness to the man with her) so that in her mind it became possible to come to terms with what had happened, back there, outside camp, and think of it as a beginning and not an end. Sickening, terrible, it had been: colleagues, friends, a man whose bed she had shared, ruthlessly cut down and slaughtered — why, for God's sake? Why, to someone, had it seemed necessary?

When, after an hour, they halted for a rest, a drink, something to eat, she asked him — why?

They were in a narrow gully, out of the wind; had used their torches sparingly to find themselves places to sit, side by side, backs against eroded walls of packed sand. Had had a drink of water, and were chewing dried apricots.

"There doesn't have to be a reason," he said. "Not one, at any rate, that says 'because of this: that'. Given the opportunity, and a nod from higher authority, a lot of men have it in them to be wanton killers. It's the way most of us are made."

That, to her, was too simplistic by half, but she said nothing and thought about it. After the events of the last two days a number of given ideas, formerly accepted on trust, did indeed seem to her now to be wholly irrelevant, that was a fact, and all that had gone before part of some juvenile dream, or charade, played out in circumstances bearing little relation to reality. The only reality that mattered, *out here*, was of another kind: a world wholly inimical (or at best uncaring) and in contention with that world a man and a woman alone, come together for the purposes of survival: their weapons, their defences, only those they carried with them or of their own manufacture, nothing else. The truth? Maybe. If so, what hope was there, in the long run? None. Unthinkable, and the mind refused to admit that either . . . "We are created in God's image, so they say," she murmured, by way of reply.

"You're religious?" he asked. "You have a faith?"

"No."

"Neither have I," he said.

★ ★ ★

By using the stars and his compass, Andersen got them to the vicinity of Budeiya around midnight: the ruined village somewhere within half a mile or so in one direction or another, but no sense in trying to find it, or enter it, until daylight. They found a hollow which gave some protection from the wind, wrapped their blankets around them, and lay down on the big sheet of plastic that he had brought with him to serve as a groundsheet. Slept fitfully, after a time, the sleep of exhaustion, rolling together, for warmth, as the night wore on. Woke soon after first light, chilled to the bone, stiff and aching, their blankets and hair wet with dew.

The ancient walls of the village were not five hundred yards off, pale yellow mud-brick, cracked and leaning, the occasional palmhead and spikey acacia showing above them. No sign of life over there, or in the desert anywhere round about, carefully and hard though they looked; nothing moved. He stood up, stretched, blew on his hands, and grinned at her. Said, "Well, there it is. Home, for a day or two. Provided it's as empty as it looks."

"We'll stay?" she asked curiously. She was running on the spot, in quick bursts, to loosen up and get her circulation going.

"Mm, until the hue and cry dies down, I hope. Until everyone comes to believe that we're lost in the desert, disappeared without trace."

"There's water?"

"With luck."

"I have to have a pee," she said quietly glancing at him. "Excuse me — "

"I'll see you in a moment," he said, and moved away a short distance, to do the same himself. Turned and rejoined her after a suitable interval. In silence they gathered their things together, and set off, across the sand. Across ridged 'plots' that a long time ago, when the climate had been different in these parts, perhaps, had been cultivation. Leaving tracks, footprints, behind them for all to see. After walking a little way she drew his attention to them, saying, "If anyone comes looking they'll know where to find us, won't they?"

"By midday they'll be gone," he said. "Before then, if the wind gets up."

She nodded, and they went on. Entered the village by an alleyway between head-high walls, heaps of sand, tumbled mud-brick and other debris underfoot and on either side, with the occasional desert plant — cactus, camel-thorn — poking through here and there. Picking their way, and keeping a sharp lookout, they headed in, looking for the mosque and, more vitally, a well. A still-usable well. A village like this one had been, small and isolated, could never have relied for its water on falaj or qa'nat: there was nowhere within twenty miles of it from which underground channels might conceivably have been dug; so a well, or wells, there must have been, once.

They stood in the small square of the

village, their packs at their feet, looking about them. The sun low in the sky still, deep orange, and no great heat in it, for an hour or two yet; but the need for shade, shelter, as vital to them as anything else if they were to stay here any length of time. The mosque facing them, a building, what was left of it, a little larger than any other they had seen so far: they crossed the hard-packed sand of the square, ducked to enter by the low arched doorway, still intact, and went inside. Sand piled within, smoothly climbing the walls to the height of niches cut into them all round — but the roof gone and no shelter there. They went out again and tried somewhere else: another building, close by, this one with the ends of heavy beams still protruding from its walls, cracked and bleached by time, above head-height. And, this time, they were in luck —

A small 'room,' perhaps twelve by eight in total, and a good half of it still roofed over: the beams, of rough-hewn timber, supporting a ceiling of mud and matting. Shelter indeed, if what was left would only hold a little longer. Carefully, letting his eyes become accustomed, first, to the shadow, Andersen reached up and tried the ceiling here and there with his hands. Dust, bits of plaster and matting, fell to the floor, bits of matting came loose, but there was still certainly a little strength remaining, enough perhaps to hold it in place till the next rains. He smiled at her, wiping a hand over his face, and then they inspected the rest of the room. A mess of fallen timber, blown sand and bits of matting, but nothing they couldn't clear away, or use. "Not bad," he said. But then, seriously, "One thing only. If we're going to stay here, watch out for crawlies, scorpions, camel-spiders, maybe there aren't any, but they could still be around. They like this sort of place." He stared up at the ceiling again, for sign of nests, but could see none.

She nodded, looking about her. Camel-spiders particularly — she had only seen one once — but the mere thought of them filled her with horror: their method of feeding on living flesh one of the nightmares of nature. She hadn't thought of the possibility of camel-spiders, until now.

"Let's have a look, out back," he said.

And when they went through, into what had once been a yard behind the house, it was there: a well. Over against a broken-down wall in one corner, in the shade of a big acacia. A *known* well, one that had been protected from drifting sand over the years, the low mortared ring of stone about its mouth covered over with warped planking and dry palm-fronds. *Not* recently cut, he could see that, which was important, so that it was possible that while this well was indeed known it was also very little used, nowadays anyway. The sort of risk which they might have to take, in the days ahead, not once but again and again. He only prayed, fervently, that it still contained water. Began tossing aside branches and planking, to take a look, and she came to kneel down at his side to help.

Done, and leaning forward together, they peered down into the depths: but there was nothing to be seen down there, only darkness. He looked round for a stone, and found one, a yard or two away, a small rounded pebble. Returned to the well-side and leaned down again, lower, turning his head so that he might catch the smallest sound from below; then dropped it in. After a time a very faint splash. Truly: water. He sat back and laughed with relief, and she with him. But she sobered quickly, and said, "So all right, but how do we get it?"

"I'll show you," he said, and rose to his feet. Recrossed the yard and went back inside the house. Reappeared a minute later, with an aluminium billycan, a thin towel, and a ball of strong nylon twine. "I came prepared," he said.

She shook her head, but said nothing. Returned with him to the well: on the way he gathered up another stone, larger than the one he had used before. While she watched, he wrapped the stone in the towel, knotting the four corners tightly together to hold it in; then unravelled a long length of twine and tied the end of it to the sling he had made. Finally swung the weighted towel out over the wellhead and began running the twine through his hands to lower it in. Twenty, thirty, maybe thirty-five feet, before the twine went slack. He let the towel soak in water for a moment or two, down there, and then quickly began to draw it in again, hand over hand.

She grabbed the billycan and knelt beside him, ready; when the towel came up reached out quickly to catch the water dripping from it. Together they brought towel and billy to the well-side, and he squeezed out all the water from the towel that he could between his hands. Half a canful. Like manna from Heaven. In the wilderness, life. He raised the billy and smelt it, nodded, but said, "We better not drink this as it is — we can wash with it, though, and keep cool. When we need to we can boil it, and it should be OK after that."

She stared at him briefly across the billycan of water, but then looked away. Wanting to say many things, to thank him (for her very existence) and say she was with him, but for the moment the words wouldn't come. Emotions long atrophied within her for want of use — if she had ever really known them — struggling to find some form of expression, some form that did not finally commit her, to him or anyone else. Useless. She *was* committed, and regretted that not at all, now. So stood up and when he rose also and faced her, sensing her mood, reached out with both her hands and held him by the shirt, just held him like that, looking down. Said finally, her mind made up but words coming slowly, "Life's too short, maybe, for us to waste time, in meaningless pretence. So I'm ready for you, know that." She looked up. "Please don't rush me, that's all."

He didn't catch on for a moment; then did. Said quietly, "My life is in your hands."

7

HE had gone to reconnoitre the rest of the village and, while he did so, she unpacked and began getting their house in order. At first spent a lot of time with her heart in her mouth, seeing crawlies everywhere, but soon got over that: there didn't appear to be any. A 'broom' of some kind was her first requirement and she managed this with a piece of old matting which she rolled up and held in her hand, sweeping out the floor of the room under the ceiling that remained until it was clear of plaster and rubbish. Then laid their piece of plastic over it, and on that spread out the things they had brought with them, in rucksack and sack: his here, hers there. Saw immediately that he had brought almost no spare clothing with him, socks, a pair of sneakers, that

125

was all: had concentrated entirely on essentials, or what might be essentials, with one exception, a half-bottle of whisky, which delighted her. To be used strictly for medicinal purposes, of course!

As she had, he had brought two litre-canteens of water; one of these was now less than half-full. Powdered milk, dried egg, tea, saccharine; a dozen packets of soup, two cans of bully-beef; dried fruit and split peas, rice; only the bully-beef heavy in comparison with the goodness it contained. With what she had carried with her — more of the same, with exceptions — they would eat pretty well, she thought, for some time. Thinking things out as she went along, she replaced all foodstuffs in her emptied rucksack; then found a forked acacia-branch outside by the well, stripped it of bark and, returning to the room, leant it against the wall in one corner; hung the rucksack and its contents from it. Settled down again on the floor to check over their other supplies: two plastic plates, plastic mugs and spoons, a kitchen knife (fairly sharp); matches, four boxes, cigarettes, two packets (both full); six stubby candles. She went out again, found a short length of board not too badly warped and, with it and a few chunks of mud-brick of roughly the same size, improvised a low table against the wall, close to 'the larder', in the area of the room which she had already designated as the one in which they would sit and eat. On it laid out the smokes and other things; stood the whisky and canteens of water beside. Tools next: a small axe-head and a lightweight mattock or digging-tool, both lacking hafts; it was while she was thinking about these, applauding the forethought of the man who had brought them, that she heard him coming back. Went to the doorway out into the square, to meet him.

He was dragging half a dozen freshly cut palm-fronds, leafy-green and resilient, and was dripping with sweat from his exertions. Smiled at her as he let them fall to the ground. "Plenty more where these came from," he said. "Bedding."

"You're too much," she said, and meant it, with all her heart. Led the way inside and poured him out a mug of water. He sat down, his back against the wall, and drank it, slowly, letting his eyes wander over what she had done, so far, with the room. Nodded approvingly, and said, "You know, between us, we don't make a bad team."

"I hope so," she said, but was obviously pleased, relieved, to hear him say it. She folded herself down onto the floor, facing him, and reached across to the table for a pack of cigarettes and matches. Said, "We could allow ourselves one of these, don't you think?"

"Why not."

She lit two and passed one across, and for half a minute they smoked in silence, with deep enjoyment. After a while he said, "When we've finished this, and before the real heat comes, why don't we clear the rest of this room, all that rubbish, then make a fire and have some food."

"Okay," she said. "Let's do it together." Then asked, "But shouldn't we stand watch, one of us?"

"I don't think so," he said. "Doesn't really serve much purpose. If anyone comes they'll know pretty soon we're around. The main thing is not to show ourselves outside the village, and not to show a light, at night. We do all our cooking during daylight hours. With dry wood there'll be no smoke."

She nodded, accepting it. Then lay down on the floor, pillowing her head on a blanket while she finished her cigarette. Sighed once in contentment. After a time reached out, a little hesitantly, and gave him her hand. Briefly he pressed it, hard, before raising it to his lips.

★ ★ ★

In the cool of afternoon they washed, with water from the well. Had drawn a canful together first, then — openly appraising each others' bodies as they were revealed — stripped off, and used a scarf of hers to sponge each other down. Moving on from there to soap one another, to examine and caress, so that the delight which they experienced in offering their bodies one to the other should be prolonged and their hands familiar with the shape and symmetry of all that was theirs, before the blind agony that they looked for in consummation. He was beautifully built, hugely strong, she had never handled a man before whose physical advantage over her was half so formidable, and revelled in his brute-maleness, in a daze of longing and — as time passed — of submission. She in turn, to him, was of a long-limbed perfection that he had never previously encountered, her physique slender, supple, yet hard as a whip, and he was torn between a kind of madness

130

that drove him to maul her, tear her to pieces with his hands while, at the same time, he knew that to be anything but gentle with her was unthinkable. Curiously, reverently, they discovered one another; then came together in a close embrace that signified that thus far everything had gone supremely well; and immediately he lifted her and carried her inside.

Where he put her down, on the soft bed of palm-leaves they had together prepared, she spread herself, legs wide, arms behind her head, and waited for him, challenging him with her eyes. Afraid that their wonderful beginning might yet end in disillusion.

But then, as he came down to her, and continued arousing her with mouth and hands, found herself very quickly losing control of muscle and limb, could only moan and utter small cries of encouragement, until he entered her. Surfaced then for a little while, her eyes dilated, her body on fire, as he filled her and stroked her within, as he gripped her hands and held her still — until, too quickly, the darkness gathered and she could see him no more, and surrendered entirely to the rising tide that held them both in thrall, crushing her, breaking her; and cried out, dying a little death, dying slowly, his full weight upon her, his words of adoration in her ears . . . Aware, as she recovered her senses, of feelings of bewilderment and near-terror; these overlaid at once by the realisation that she had rarely, if ever, known it so good, had given, and been given, everything, for the first time (perhaps) in her life: her joy and acknowledgement of this overwhelming her, a second time, so that she burst into tears, of gratitude and release. They kissed then, lingeringly; held one another, eyes closed, breathing gradually returning to normal; and during that short period of time became, truly, lovers.

★ ★ ★

It dawned on them both almost immediately that these two days they would spend at Budeiya, hopefully undisturbed, were bound to constitute a high point in their lives. After Budeiya a wider world, with all its hazards and opportunities, would have to be faced, but for these two days there was only themselves. In that time, in a blaze of happiness, they set out to get to know each other — as far as any individual may ever know another — and forget everything else.

Sexually they were evenly matched, without hang-ups or inhibitions of any kind: what one wanted, the other gave. To her, if you loved, this was completely natural; to him, with his more limited experience of the opposite sex, something new, a freedom it took him a little while to accustom himself to. Not long, under her tuition, and with her wholehearted consent: exploring together the whole gamut of physical excitation, from controlled savagery to tenderness, to the very limit of what their feelings for one another would allow; until, for them, there was nothing left and gradually a pattern of courtship and loving that suited them best began to emerge.

So, to the second day, after one of their bouts of near-frenzied copulation: they lay on their bed in the cool of early evening, exhausted, the sweat drying on their bodies, and she said, "I have nothing, to stop myself having a child. I didn't think. It's bound to happen, sooner or later, if we go on like this. Does it matter?"

He shook his head, watching her. Said, "All that matters is that you should want one. If you do, let it happen. Would it please you, a child of mine?"

"Oh yes." Her words the ultimate compliment to him.

"We have to make it to Abu Khim within a fortnight," he said. "If we don't it's highly unlikely there'll be anyone there to meet us."

She sat up, combing her fingers through her tangled hair. Asked him, "Tell me, what is 'Abu Khim'? Why are we going there?"

"I don't know what kind of place it is," he said. "Except that it's by the ocean. Maybe a village, maybe a headland only. It's where the radar people from the Hajjar are instructed to make for and where they will be picked up."

"Radar people?" She stretched out again, reaching for a canteen of water on the table, and he ran a hand caressingly down her spine, making her catch her breath.

"Mm. There's a big group of them, radar and construction people and their families, up in the mountains at a place called Gumsa — a hush-hush project. The navy will get them out from Ras Abu Khim. That's their only way of escape."

"And we? We'll join up with them, is that what you hope?" She drank and passed the canteen over to him, and he

135

sat up to take it. Drank in his turn.

"We'll make for Gumsa in the first instance," he said. "Join them if they're still there. If not, follow them to the sea."

She lay down again, her head in his lap, looking up at him. Asked, "You think we'll make it?"

He laughed. "We've every chance," he said. "You'll see."

Part Two

Trial of Strength

8

SEIFUDDIN was an old man now, and over the years his stature had decreased. In addition he had an arthritic hip which gave him hell in the early mornings, and his left eye, which had never been good, had almost no vision left. None of which prevented him from exercising the same ruthless dominance over his region as he had done now for nearly ten years. He and his people, the Bani Qasim, were the chosen of God, he manipulated them by rules whose origins and devious complexity were both lost in the mists of time; anyone else, other tribes, other peoples, were to him little better than vermin. When they were within his reach and useful to him he tolerated them; when they were out of reach, he paid them no attention at all; when they displeased him — and happened to be within his power — he dealt with them, sooner or later, in ways that often meant that they were never heard of again. He was not a pleasant man, since the death of his son, and was both hated in some quarters and generally feared. That he employed the persuasions of torture, and took a pleasurable interest in such matters himself, was only one of the numerous vile charges levelled against him but never proved. He *was*, and one day he would die or be replaced, but even that not a few people, and they weren't all simple-minded, had begun to doubt. He existed, and always would.

He had an office in the Sharia Courts building in old Kamil, but seldom used it; preferred to conduct affairs from his own home or that of one of his close relatives. Wherever he was or went was always surrounded by men who owed him everything, one-time slaves many of them, others from families so insignificant that he was their only hope of advancement of any kind. Thus, on a certain day in high summer, he was in the area of the town known as Jash', renowned for the quality of its dates; had stayed several nights at the house of a cousin; and now, late morning and the room warmed already by the sun, sat cross-legged in his host's majlis, hearing reports, issuing directives, dispensing favour and occasionally cash from the strong-box at his side, to any whom his minions permitted into his presence. Seated by himself down one end of the long room, a spare grey man, clean-shaven apart from a wisp of beard, his white thobe worn loose; his four bodyguards armed with modern rifles some distance away so that, unless voices were raised, they were out of earshot. The man to whom he was presently whispering, who sat cross-legged before him, leaning forward to catch his words, a man of the desert, his dark saturnine face betraying no sign of emotion. A man called Tariki, whose mission, two days before, had been the destruction of the encampment

141

at Ayoun and the massacre of all foreigners working there.

Already Tariki had described how the massacre had been carried out, as ordered, and had gone over everything which had taken place — but concluded that, regrettably, two members of the team out there, both Europeans, had escaped. He made a small gesture, quickly, as his master glared at him, to let the old man know that there was more to be told. Went on to say that the two missing faranji had been tracked down, to the old village of Budeiya, which was where they were now, in hiding.

For a few seconds Seifuddin said nothing. Then, sibilantly, "If you know where they are, what has stayed your hand? Why have they not been dealt with, like the rest?"

"I thought," Tariki said meaningfully, "that since they chose to travel *that* way, you may perhaps prefer to let them die."

"They have a vehicle with them?"

"No. They are on foot."

"Do they know that you have discovered their whereabouts?"

"Again no. For a certainty, not."

Slowly the old man nodded, his mind at work: thinking that indeed there was a well at Budeiya, but that soon enough the two fugitives would be forced to move, in search of food. Truly it might be interesting to see, what two faranji did, how they planned to survive, in the wilderness. Their sufferings, their struggles — and he himself poised to snuff out their efforts at any time, from day to day — truly there might be a certain amusement to be derived from such sport. Finally he asked, "Who are they, these two?"

"One is the soldier who looked after the camp, the other is a woman."

"The soldier, indeed," Seifuddin murmured, his eyes closing to mask any expression they might reveal. "That one I have met, I think."

"Yes, him."

"Good," the old man said briefly,

looking up again. Added, "Ya-Tariki, you have done well, and I shall remember it. Go now and return to Budeiya and keep watch with your men day and night. When the faranji move follow them and bring word to me. Bring word of where they go and everything they do. Do not let them know that you are watching them. Do not ever let them know that."

"Ya-Sidi," Tariki said, touched his forehead in token of fealty, and got to his feet.

9

THEY could see the lights of Kamil in the distance. Had marched for two nights to get where they were, and were worn out. Spent the last hour before dawn huddled in their blankets under the low bank of some wadi, one of them keeping watch while the other slept. Then, when there was light enough to see, lugged their packs a little way along the wadi-side until they found a stony gully leading out of it which, provided they kept down, would protect them from passing eyes. There was a bit of shelter from the sun also, from a stunted eucalyptus tree, and this was as important as anything else. He spread their blankets on the rocky ground; they lay down and had a drink of water and something to eat. Then he took the first watch while she flaked out once more.

Slowly, very slowly, the day passed, the heat mounting inexorably towards midday, slackening off gradually towards afternoon and evening. That they were so tired was in fact a help to them; at least, for some hours and in turn, they passed periods of time in oblivion. Sleeping or waking, flies tormented them; in the heat lizards appeared from under rocks to lie basking nearby; once a big eagle spotted them and circled for an hour but did not stoop or attack, before flying off; for a while, across the wadi, camels could be seen browsing in the low trees and scrub, apparently unattended. No human being came near them, that they caught sight of, nor did they hear any vehicle pass, either close by or in the distance.

Nevertheless, he suspected they were being followed: that someone was on their trail and that, from time to time, they were being watched. Why this feeling had come to him he didn't know — since leaving Budeiya they hadn't seen a living soul — the fact remained, and stayed with him, that someone was back there, and after them. The Bedouin: as a serving soldier in this part of the world he knew something of the Bedus' almost uncanny affinity with this sort of environment, and ability to use that environment to his own advantage: knew enough not to dismiss the fears he had the slightest bit lightly. Perhaps, years ago, he had acquired a little of that same affinity himself and the skills that went with it, which was an added reason for believing that his fears might not be unfounded, mere products of his imagination. Across the wadi there was nothing to be seen; when he got to his feet, very slowly and carefully — and Lina lying stretched out at his feet — the plains around Kamil to north and south appeared empty, but that did not mean that they were empty in reality. Of his suspicions, though, he said nothing, either then or later, the hardship and discomfort the two of them were undergoing together quite enough for her to cope with, he thought, for the time being.

Not that she complained, or gave the slightest indication that the heat and suffering of this day — a second day — were getting her down. With him she appeared to take everything in her stride: with him, that was the key. The 'honeymoon' they had shared together at Budeiya still with her, so that — far more so than he — the outside world held for her, for the time being, very little importance. A mood, a condition, which he could only pray would stay with her a while longer, and which he did his best to sustain: giving her the physical contact that she could not now do without, remaining cheerful, without overdoing it, and hopeful at all times. No hardship for him in fact, because he loved her and her love for him gave him the humility required.

As the long day drew to its close they repacked the few things they had taken from their packs, had a long drink of water and a little food, then lay down side by side on their blankets to wait

148

for the night. "No more days, like this," he said.

"It wasn't so bad."

"Bad enough," he murmured.

★ ★ ★

To enter the old part of Kamil, with its labyrinth of narrow alleyways between the sleeping houses, would have been to invite disaster. Luckily they didn't have to do so to find the house they were looking for: Hafez, one-time Embassy driver in the capital, had used a major portion of his retirement-gratuity to build himself a more 'modern' home in the newer, Qasma, area of the town. Here houses, their walled compounds and small enclosed gardens, were not cheek by jowl but scattered without apparent plan about the desert, built usually of concrete blocks, and though trees had been planted here and there between them none had reached anything approaching maturity yet . . . Around midnight they crossed the main road, circled a little to get their bearings and then entered Qasma from the south, using their torches now to light their way from time to time. The night silent about them, the open spaces between each compound empty of people: a big light here and there over a painted metal gate, the sand underfoot often deeply rutted by the passage of wheeled traffic. They walked on: a dog barked some distance away, and there was a chill dusty-smelling breeze in their faces; passed the wrecks of two jeeps, stripped of all useful parts, and a small cantina with a busted fridge on its stoep, its walls covered with Pepsi and Mirinda signs and doors closed. Walked further in, till they reached the mosque, in daytime the open ground before it a meeting-place and casual market, where Andersen halted. Looking about him he said, "On the left there, I think, the first house you come to." During his stay at Ayoun he had visited the old driver once, but once only: on that occasion had been welcomed and made much of by the old man and his family. What he sought now from the old driver was still a lot to ask, he knew it, and could well put the family in danger. There were times, nevertheless, when such things had to be done.

He led the girl round the walls of Hafez' small domain, until he found the entrance, a metal double-door set in a metal frame up two steps, with a bulkhead light above it. Used a coin from his pocket to rap on one of the metal panels, the sound cutting into the silence of the night but without reverberation. The silence continued and he rapped again. Beside him Lina said quietly, "Maybe they won't answer, it's so late."

"Give them time," he murmured. "Give them time," and rapped again.

Suddenly there was a stirring inside house and compound, and voices raised, somewhere in an interior room. A door opened and slammed closed, and sandalled feet approached the outside door: a man holding a lantern; Andersen could see him, a little, through the crack between one door and the other: a dark figure, grumbling to himself. Then a voice, irritably, "Who is it? What do you want? In the name of God — ?"

"I am Andersen-Sah'b," he said, his mouth close to the crack. "I come to you because I need help. I am Andersen-Sah'b, from Ayoun, and I have a woman with me."

Silence again. Then inside the house more voices, as other members of the family roused themselves and came to the outer door. A baby began to cry somewhere, but very fortunately there did not appear to be a dog. He heard a voice, that of the man who had come to the door first, say, "He says he is 'Andersen-Sah'b', from Ayoun, the one who came, that day: the Embassy-Sah'b."

Hafez took over then. Said, through the crack, "If you are Andersen-Sah'b, speak to me, that I may hear your

152

voice. If you have a light shine it in your face."

He did as he was told. Saying quietly, "Hafez, old friend, you can see now, it is I. Look, it is I, is it not?" He took off his hat. "I beseech you, that we may enter, and that you tell your family to keep their voices down."

No further delay then. Bolts were drawn back and one half of the door swung creaking open. They went in, taking their packs with them, and it was immediately shut and bolted again behind them. By the light of the lantern he shook hands all round with the men and boys awaiting them, blankets over their shoulders; introduced Lina to them, his wife.

"Come," the old man said. "The night is cold. Let us go in. We can talk in greater comfort inside." So far, Andersen thought, the thing had gone as well as he had dared to hope and he prayed only that it might continue to do so.

To the left of the main doorway

was the family's reception-room, and it was there they were led. There was electricity, lighting from a single hanging light-bulb, rugs upon the floor and cushions against the walls. They unlaced and took off their boots, and then sat down side by side; across the room the old man, his brother and their several sons took their places facing them. A younger boy brought glasses of water and a tray of dates while greetings, already exchanged at the door, were repeated. Then Andersen explained immediately their appearance, travel-worn, dirty, their clothes stained and slept-in, by saying, only, for the moment, that they had come far and on foot.

"My house is yours," the old man said quietly. "That you should take rest here and be welcome. There has been trouble, I think."

"Much trouble," Andersen said. "Where we came from, Ayoun, people have died and only the two of us escaped."

"The country is in ferment," the old man agreed. "So we hear on the radio. There is warfare and many have died in the fighting — "

"It still goes on?"

"It grows worse, from day to day; But, may God be praised, it has not reached Kamil yet."

"Pray it may never do so," Andersen said.

Silence then, as refreshment was taken and cigarettes lit. Beside him, as he lit hers for her, Lina smiled at him wearily and then lay back against the cushions, resting, wisely, until it should be time to make another move. After a few moments Andersen looked up and said, "Ya-Hafez, what we need now more than anything else is a vehicle."

The old man hesitated, a fraction of a second. Then asked, "But, where will you go?"

"There is a place," Andersen said. Deliberately he did not name Ras Abu Khim. "A place from which it is arranged that all faranji will be picked up. You know how these things are, in emergencies, the Embassy has plans, to safeguard the lives of British people. But that place is very far from here, we cannot hope to reach it on foot, in time. If we tried we would certainly arrive too late."

The old man nodded. "Such things I remember, yes." Then, "And a jeep is no problem. There is either mine or my son's" — he gestured to the young man on his right, the same who had first met them at the main doors. "It will be no trouble, for my son to drive you, to wherever you want to go. There is no shortage of petrol yet, in Kamil, I am glad to say."

"I am deeply grateful," Andersen said. "Nevertheless" — carefully, he went on — "the thing cannot be done that way. Your son would be risking his life on our behalf, and that I cannot permit. What I had in mind was to *buy* one of your vehicles. I came prepared and have much money with me, enough to give you a good price." He straightened where he sat, watched the row of men opposite him: young and old, they exchanged glances, looked down, looked away, waiting for Hafez, the senior member of the family, to give his judgment. On the next few minutes, and what was said during that time, their survival depended, in all probability, Andersen knew.

"Let us think the matter over," the old man said. "Let us rest the night and make a decision in the morning."

"No," Andersen said. "I beg you to understand, and forgive, my haste, but we must be on our way, tonight. Be away from Kamil before dawn. The longer we stay the more risk there will be, to you and your family."

"You are being followed?" The old man's eyes glinted.

"No," immediately. "No one knows where we are." The lie — if it was a lie, as he felt fairly certain it was, a betrayal that would remain with him, on his conscience, for the rest of his life. So be it; he accepted that as the price to be paid, a very small one by comparison with the price this old man and his family might be asked to pay, because of it, which was likely to be infinitely greater. Sometimes, when the chips were down, a man had to choose, between his own life (and that of someone he loved) and those of others, and he, Andersen, was no saint. He only hoped and prayed that his denial had sounded convincing enough.

After a while, and sadly — as though, in a way, he knew, and even understood — the old man said, "All right, one of our jeeps is yours. When we have taken coffee, let us go, round the back, that is where the garage is."

"I thank you, with all my heart," Andersen said.

10

SHE had the strongest possible sensation of taking off, and that life was opening out, full of infinite possibilities. That there was nothing now to stop them achieving their goal. The road they were on was narrow, dusty, stony, hardly a road at all, but it was rising, always rising, towards the heights. After that would come the high plateau of the northern Hajjar, plain sailing on the whole, they hoped, before the long descent to the sea. But the sea a long way off, no need to think about that now; now was for the enjoyment of the way ahead, in the early morning, and freedom, and winning through. She felt happier, gut-happier, than she ever remembered being, even as a child, physically and emotionally surfeited, complete (at last) and ready for anything: the man at her side, driving, *hers*, a fellow human-being not to be compared with any other, someone with whom all might be shared, whose joy she could contrive and make her own. And when trouble came, as it surely would, misunderstandings, set-backs, illness, these too to be faced together, and endured, mastered, come through. Oh, but she was so damned excited, and in the car found it difficult to contain her euphoria.

Their dress, it was now Arab-style, purchased from the old Embassy driver and his family at Kamil: thobes, of the winter sort — for the high mountains were ahead — dark brown and of heavyweight cotton, belted at the waist, and on their feet were sandals made from old vehicle tyres. Their heads, those a problem, always, from now on, but they had done their best to disguise those also: their headcloths arranged to show no glimpse of telltale hair and folded across the lower part of the face, against dust, so that only the eyes and bridge of the nose were visible. Tremendous: they looked like a couple of the most desperate sort of bandit, she thought, and she would have to remember, when on foot, to use her body like a man's, gesture like a man, and pitch her voice low, whenever they were in the company of strangers: a part that she would really relish playing.

They travelled on through the foothills, above them the towering bergs of gleaming red igneous rock, the road, worsening, with low scrub either side, scarcely wide enough in places now to allow the jeep to pass. With dangerous boulder-strewn drops from time to time on one hand or the other, that became deep chasms as they climbed further in, so that great care and occasionally panache were needed. Five gallons of petrol, or thereabouts, was all they had: not enough to take them all the way, but to the radar-station at Gumsa, yes, enough for that. If all went well —

If. Twenty miles out of Kamil and

the sun beginning to throw steep slanting shadows across the valleys, they rounded a bend — a sheer drop to their right, a sheer cliff-face to their left — and came upon a landslip completely blocking the road. Andersen drew up a few yards from it, and they sat studying it, without speaking, before getting down: a great sloping pile of broken rock and scree, uprooted bushes and powdery sand. No way round and some of the fallen boulders, what they could see of them, of a size and weight beyond the capability of human hands to shift without help of machinery. He spread out his map on the hot bonnet of the jeep and she came and put her arm across his shoulders to study it with him. Another 'road' up into the mountains; there was no other alternative, they had to find one, if one existed. Such was her state of mind that she didn't doubt for one moment that the possibility was there.

And so it proved: there *was* another track marked, but it began eight or ten miles back; she remembered it now, a trail leading off right down a long valley and an abandoned Bedu encampment in the distance: a trail which — according to the map — swung wide to the east and climbed into the Jebel Hajjar by a route nearly parallel to the one they had been following. So all right, that trail they would have to take, while they had petrol in the tank it was unthinkable that they should try anything else. He kissed her, caressed her; she laughed, welcoming him, and they made love at the roadside — sharp stones stabbing into her rump, but who cared? — and when they were done got back into the jeep once more.

He turned the car with some difficulty and when they were on the road again, heading back the way they had come, she put her head on his shoulder and dozed fitfully, as the nature of the road allowed, for several miles. Sad to be going back, down again, but it didn't matter; nothing did. She had never before, she thought, felt able to entrust her life, her well-being, so totally into the hands of anyone else, as seemed wholly natural to her now, in present circumstances; and could only marvel at the changes the last few days had surely wrought in her. Hard, cynical *grasping* creature that she had been, in truth — she knew it — where was that creature now? Vanished without trace, it seemed, and hopefully for ever . . .

After they had travelled eight miles or so, so that it couldn't be far now to the turn-off, they met another vehicle for the first time, a light van, coming up. The road again narrow at that point, and no room to pass.

Jeep and van halted, twenty yards of dusty trail between them, and she saw that in the cab of the other vehicle there was one person only, a boy in fact, no more than eighteen, or so it was revealed, when he got out: a slim youth in a faded shirt and patched jeans, someone's driver, perhaps, on a delivery run to some village higher up from one of the dukas at Kamil. Motioning her to stay where she was, Andersen got out, and man and boy met half-way between the two vehicles, to sort matters out. Shook hands; and then the scene unfolding before her eyes as though part of some dreadful nightmare: horrifying, unjustifiable, and yet, after the first shock, she revelled in it, her body and senses reacting atavistically, with savage pleasure.

Andersen speaking to the boy, the two standing close, and then the man's knee, viciously, into the boy's genitals and as his head came down a single smashing blow from the man's fist that lifted the boy off the ground and hurled him back down the trail, probably already half-dead. Never mind, the big man upon him, pinning him to the ground, arm rising, flailing down, beating the boy's head in with a stone — until it was inconceivable that there could be life left. Death of a boy unknown, at the roadside.

She got out, shaking, not looking either at the corpse or at Andersen's face, as he rose to his feet and turned to watch her come up. Then made herself look at him: his eyes narrow, feral, as gradually his breathing quietened and he began massaging one hand with the other. After a moment, quietly, he said, as if the thing needed explaining, "We want his petrol, and anything else he may have."

"Yes." She nodded, and looked away. Then went slowly to the body, stared down at it for a few seconds, her hands at her mouth.

11

WHEN they had stripped the van of anything useful to them, and syphoned the petrol from the tank, Andersen put the boy's body back into the cab; then, using the slope, they let the van run back to the edge of the road and tipped her over. She didn't fall far, ten, fifteen yards only, where she hung in some rocks, back wheels spinning, on her side. When the dust had settled, they got back into their jeep and drove on, for a time in silence.

Came to the turning soon enough, hard left, and took it: beginning to climb once more towards the heights. But stopped again very soon: the boy had had a flask of tea with him in his cab, and they thought they would drink it, while it was still hot, but didn't get down from the jeep to do so.

"I'm totally with you," she said. "What happened back there. It's important that you know."

"You say that now," he said, not looking at her. "But would *you* have done it, in my place?"

"If I'd had your presence of mind and physical strength, yes."

"You're sure?"

"Yes. Quite sure."

"Thank God," he said. But then, "But what if I told you I enjoyed doing it? That enjoyment, of that kind, is part of me?"

"I'd believe you, up to a point," she said. "What I would not believe is that because that enjoyment is part of you you have to go looking for it, that you *thrive* on stimulation of that kind."

He gave her his free hand; turned his head and stared at her, his eyes dark. Said, "Forgive me, my Lina, if you can, in advance. There are so many ways in which I can hurt *you*, and I will do it, and take pleasure in so doing, at the time."

She pressed his hand once, hard, still watching him. Said quietly, "Do not be so naive as to think that I am any different. My weapons are more subtle, perhaps, that's all."

* * *

The road now, the new trail, was even more difficult than the other, very steep in places, little used. Nevertheless it had once surely been aligned and cut with wheeled traffic in mind and, given great care, was not impassable. Very hard going though, with much use of low-ratio, very tiring, and by midday they had had enough, had to let their vehicle take a break and cool down. Though her engine sounded good, she was old, her shocks and suspension had seen better days, and she boiled easily if not given frequent attention. Never mind, until midday they were travelling in the direction they wanted to go, and their mood was one of renewed confidence and occasionally exhilaration. By midday they had covered nearly fifteen miles on the new road, and halted by a narrow waterfall at an altitude of around two thousand feet. Got out and stretched wearily, physically spent and in need of food and rest.

Back the way they had come, through gaps in the mountains, over serried ranks of foothills, they could see the desert plains they had left, hazed in sunlight; a few miles ahead of them, higher yet, was the first village they expected to come to, Wadi Saim. So far, in all their travels that day — with the exception of that boy — they hadn't seen a living soul, no animal, only the occasional eagle floating in the blue. Such isolation, such quiet, when the engine was switched off, it was almost uncanny. Uncanny, and very beautiful. Just the sound of the tiny waterfall, dropping from above their heads into a small basin of rock at the roadside, running away across the road in a shallow channel the water had cut for itself, and disappearing from view. Very soon there would be shade, as the sun passed its zenith.

She stripped off and had a real 'bath', under the fall, the first proper one for many days. He watched her and when she had finished did the same. After that they ate, from their replenished supplies: seated cross-legged on the ground beside the jeep. Hot, increasingly drowsy, but eager to talk still, their interest in each other insatiable, and all thought of that boy put, deliberately, behind them.

"You'll go back to your work, at Cambridge?" he asked. "When all this is over, and we're picked up?"

"Heck, I don't know," she said, looking away. "Would you like me to?" She shrugged. "All that seems like another world now, and myself, at the time, another person. Maybe you should ask me the same question about five years from today."

He shook his head, and smiled. "You surprise me. You always gave me the impression of total dedication, as though everything else was on the side."

"That was then, a week ago. Now, I think, if I were to go back to that, in the foreseeable future, I would have to be born again."

He passed her a sticky lump of dates and she took it from his hand. "That sounds pretty final," he said. "I don't think I've ever been so certain about anything."

"Vive la difference," she said quietly, narrowing her eyes at him. Then, "And you, what will you go back to, after we've made it through?"

"I have a career, of a kind," he said. "The easy thing to do would be to return to it. It gives me a great deal of what I want — "

"But — ?"

"But, now there is you, and that alters many things." He frowned a little, still studying her face. Went on, "In a strange way, I don't want this to end, because here and now I am sure

172

of you, and I doubt that I could ever be quite so sure of you again."

"Men," she said lightly. "Very strange creatures, thank Heaven."

"You think?" He laughed.

"I'm bloody certain."

Behind him, as he sat facing her, the road stretched away in a gentle curve under its wall of rock until it rounded a bend and disappeared from view. Around that bend there now appeared a Bedouin woman, in black, her face hidden by a batoola, leading a donkey. "Company," she murmured, indicating with her eyes the direction from which the woman was approaching: approaching quickly, striding out downhill, and the donkey, a bedding-roll and a load of firewood on its back, trotting after. When Andersen got to his feet and turned, awaiting the woman's arrival, she rose with him and stood at his shoulder.

Ten yards away the woman halted, pursing her lips to make hissing noises to her ass, so that it too stopped. Then,

173

from that distance, gave greeting, her eyes glinting behind her facemask.

They replied. Hesitantly the woman stepped forward, gestured to the little waterfall tumbling down the rockface to their right. Said, "Mai."

"Tafadha'li," Andersen said and, not taking her eyes off them, the woman went to the fall, cupped her hands and raised them several times to her mouth, drinking thirstily. When she had finished clicked her fingers at the donkey, calling it over to drink as well.

"Where are you from? Where are you going?" Andersen asked.

Immediately the woman seemed to relax a little, and turned to face them: poured out a stream of Arabic, shrill, heavily accented, and containing many words in dialect unknown to them, but the place-names 'Wadi Saim' and 'Kamil' — the latter repeated several times — clearly distinguishable.

"Leish Kamil?" Andersen asked. "It is many miles. It's a very long way."

The woman shrugged. Said something about her man being at Kamil, and that, in God's time, she would join him there. Not today, not tomorrow maybe, but certainly the day following.

Andersen turned away. Locked eyes with Lina's for a moment, so that she knew, without a shadow of doubt, what was in his mind, that he was considering as a serious possibility — .

"No!" she said, and put a hand on his arm.

"I have to," he murmured. "We *can't* let her go."

"We *must*." She saw the danger well enough, of course she did, of letting this woman continue her journey; still, to take another life, so soon after the other, simply wasn't on. If he acted now, a second time, in that way, then their relationship, strong and binding though it seemed, had no chance of surviving intact, she knew it. So bent down quickly and picked up a plate on which still remained some rice and dates from their meal; called the

175

woman over, and offered the hospitality of the road.

He turned with her and, as the woman came closer, her fears receding, said — with a sigh that was at least partly relief — "All right."

★ ★ ★

"You think we're being followed?" she asked quietly, driving. "What makes you think that?"

They had passed through the village of Wadi Saim, in a long valley of palms and citrus groves — had bought goats' milk from a boy at the roadside — and were climbing again, the steep rocky gorges of the high Hajjar on all sides. Ten miles or so to go, to Gumsa which, if they were lucky, they hoped to reach before the light went.

"From the time we left Budeiya," he said. "I thought someone was on our trail, after that." He sat, feet braced, holding on to the grab-handle in the facia before him with one hand.

"But, did you see anyone?"

"No, so perhaps I was wrong."

She said nothing for a while and concentrated on her driving, which was highly demanding. Finally, after thought, she said, "If there are people out looking for us, still, it can only be because of that man at Kamil, the boss-man, what's his name — ?"

"Seifuddin," Andersen said.

"Why should it matter to him, two individuals like us, if we escape?"

He shook his head. "I don't really know, but perhaps it does. For the same reasons as made him butcher all those people at Ayoun. In a way, by our existence, we are defying his authority. Either that, or he is paying off old scores."

"Anyway," she said, "whoever was trailing us, if they were, surely we lost them, at Kamil?"

"Maybe," he said. "But I wouldn't count on it." He gestured, staring out through the windscreen at the trackless windswept ranges through which they were passing, and concluded, "Country like this may look empty but it has a thousand eyes, and word of mouth passes very quickly."

The mood he was in surprised her and was a side of him she had never seen before. She was far more inclined than he to dismiss mere 'possibilities' from her mind, and take things as they came; but perhaps too much so, she thought now, when in fact their lives were at stake. At the same time the anxieties which seemed to be afflicting him served no useful purpose: all the two of them *could* do was *get on* now and travel in hope, and in this, by allaying his fears, she could help him and thereby help them both. What *he* had done so far, at Kamil and by disposing of that boy, among other things, had taken greater toll of his resolution than she had realised, perhaps. More credit to him then, that he had done them, and the more need now of her strength, in its turn.

On impulse she pulled the jeep in to

the side of the road and stopped. When he looked at her questioningly, leaned across the front seat and kissed him on the mouth; then, as he reached for her, sat back, smiling and shaking her head, before getting out quickly. Stood a few moments beside the jeep, stretching and yawning, until he came to join her. When he did, she said, "That's enough for one day. I'm finished and so are you. Why don't we camp right here?" She looked round, searching with her eyes for a place they might get the jeep off the road. There was one such, where the road widened a little, some way ahead, before it curved out of sight.

"We can still make Gumsa today," he said.

"Why bother? Who knows what we'll find there, if anything, or anyone. Better perhaps in the morning, when we're fresh."

"Why not, then," he said.

12

SUNDOWN at Kamil, the end of a scorching hot day in high summer during which the winds from the southern deserts had driven in, blanketing the town with dust and keeping its inhabitants indoors. Cooler now, and the dust settled again, around six, when Seifuddin had himself driven to the Public Works compound on the wadi-side of Qasma; sought out there the Regional Engineer, a man of his own tribe. A figurehead, this man, without training or qualifications, his duties only to sign papers and attend meetings while others, mostly foreigners, did the work. From him Seifuddin commandeered one nearly-new bulldozer and a Sikh driver who knew his job. Briefed the driver personally in the RE's office, giving him certain instructions and laying down the law: impressing upon the man that he, Seifuddin, had been made aware that the driver had his family with him, a wife and three young children, living in the town. Only sent the Sikh away when it became apparent that the man was his slave and suitably cowed . . .

Midnight, and the gates of the Public Works enclave thrown wide by a watchman. Using the single big spotlight on the roof of his cab to see by, the Sikh crawled his charge out into the night, clanking, unsilenced exhausts backfiring and between times emitting the reverberating roar of its twin diesels. Turned her into Qasma and rolled off between the walled compounds of those who had made the place their home. Some outcry now from houses nearby, as the huge vehicle ground its way past — a furious barking of dogs — but the Sikh in his cab heard none of it, concentrating on getting the 'dozer to where he had been instructed to go, the mosque, without hitting anything *en route*. A good man, a pious man, his mind filled with horror and foreboding at what he was setting out to do; he yet saw no alternative, other than to take his own life, and what would happen to his young wife and little sons, in this terrible country, after that? His instructions were clear and had been given to him by the Ra'is himself, the dreaded Ra'is, who he had never met or seen before but of whom he had heard much. A thin old man, with one implacable eye: an eye that had warned and threatened, things a lot worse than death . . .

He reached the mosque, halted briefly in the wide open space before it, and prayed. Then, since the Deity did not answer his prayers, swivelled the spotlight above his head until it illuminated the walls of the compound that he sought. Prayed again, gritting his teeth — and then swung the 'dozer so that spotlight and bonnet both pointed the same way. Used his hydraulics to bring down his scoop, and when he had done so, leaned on his accelerator handles and gave her full power. The 'dozer surged forward: he realigned her quickly, a little more to the left, realigned her again to take the fast-approaching wall of undressed concrete blocks at rightangles, and then crashed into it. Backed off, crashed into it again, until it was down, and even he could hear screaming now. Rolled his twin tracks over the demolished wall, rocking from side to side, and set about the flimsy structures revealed to him within: smashing them down, tearing them apart — and the people in them — backing off and smashing in again, sweeping walls, roofing, debris out of the way in an orgy of destruction. Two minutes of mounting chaos, mounting frenzy — women, children running, naked, crying out to him, arms upraised in supplication — before someone, a youth, was up with him in his cab and knifed him again and again in back and neck, so that he fell headlong over his controls, and the bulldozer crawled on, like some mindless beast, away into the darkness.

So died Hafez and his brother, and three other members of the family, one child and two old women. Of the rest, two boys were badly injured and died 'in hospital' later, for want of adequate attention.

13

AFTER a good night at the roadside, quite undisturbed, they pushed on, passing by another village without stopping, and reached the high plateau of the Jebel Hajjar around eight. When they realised that they had made it, to 'the roof of the world', drew the jeep to a halt, got out and fell into one another's arms, laughing and hugging one another in jubilation: pacing about, making acquaintance with this country, this new country, to which their desperate efforts of the last few days had finally brought them. Everything was right with the world, all they had done was justified, because of this.

High open plains — over five thousand feet up — they could see for miles in every direction, the rock and sand flattened, cleared, by the action of rain and high winds over millions of years, but no wind to trouble them now, in the total calm of early morning. What luck was theirs, what supreme good fortune, to be alone together, with the beauty of space and sunrise all about them: from hence-forth nothing could stop them and the world was their oyster.

A mood which lasted them through breakfast, as they made plans. Gumsa, the radar-station there, could not be more than five miles away, just over the horizon to the north: they could see the huge dish of its scanner and massed radio beacons pointing skywards. Would there be Brits there still, or would they have all gone, summoned down to the coast? They had no way of knowing, but in any case to approach Gumsa with care, until they found out how the land lay, made obvious sense. Very likely there would be no one there, by now, but with luck they could pick up fresh supplies, tank up with petrol, before starting the long precipitous descent to the sea. So be it, and there was no point in waiting longer where they were: breakfast finished, they stowed a few things back into the jeep and prepared for departure.

But, before doing so, stood a moment looking back the way they had come, down over the jagged ranges they had negotiated that morning and the day before. In a cleft in the mountains saw the village they had passed, dark green its gardens amid the shadowy greys and browns; saw the trail by which they had ascended, snaking its way up, sometimes visible, sometimes not, clinging to the slopes of the hillsides. Aware suddenly that there were vehicles on that road, perhaps two — close together — coming up, trailing dust like drifting smoke behind them. Land Rovers, or jeeps, not trucks, and from the look of them coming hard. They watched, eyes narrowed, as the two vehicles disappeared from view, reappeared again, and kept coming;

they could not be more than half a dozen miles away, less as the crow flew. "Goddammit," Andersen said, turning. "Let's go."

They ran to the jeep, got in, and he drove, the trail ahead across rock and hard-packed gravel, hardly a trail at all, but heading, when they could see it, unmistakably in the direction of Gumsa. He was tempted to put his foot down but told himself not to be a fool — an accident now was the last thing they wanted — and kept her in third, eyes fixed on the way ahead. "Who were they?" she asked.

"No idea," he said. "But they must have come from Kamil, and they must have travelled through the night. They're either bad news or no news at all. Either way, we don't want to meet them."

"What do we do?"

He had been thinking and seconds later acted on his thoughts. Swung the jeep off the trail and headed as fast as he dared across country, looking for some dip or fold in the terrain in which they might hide: their vehicle and themselves. She clung on and, as the jolting and rocking increased — as he threw the jeep about, fighting the wheel — closed her eyes; thinking that this couldn't be right, what they were doing, risking their vehicle — for what? Two jeeps coming up, from *the direction* of Kamil, that's all they had seen: nothing, very likely nothing, to worry about. But for the moment held her peace. Maybe he knew best; certainly he knew this country and its people a lot better than she did. Nevertheless, surely, he was overreacting. Making up her mind to remonstrate with him, stop this, it was madness — very soon he would have them over — she opened her eyes and called his name . . .

But he had found the sort of place he had been looking for, a narrow fault to the terrain running at right angles to their line of flight, not deep, not difficult to take the jeep down into, but perhaps deep enough. Carefully, in low ratio, he eased the jeep down a natural incline until she stood on level ground again, and switched off, peering out through the windscreen. With luck they were just low enough to be out of sight of anyone passing on that trail back there which they had abandoned a short while before. He got out, and climbed immediately to the rim of the little depression, from where he could keep watch. She followed and came up beside him.

Five minutes passed and then the two vehicles they had seen came into view: Land Rovers, both long-wheelbase, one about fifty yards behind the other. Neither paused nor halted, both picked up speed as the terrain levelled off — they could hear the distant revving of engines hard-used — and sped on along the trail towards Gumsa. After a time disappeared from sight, their dust-clouds settling behind them. She rolled onto her back and covered her eyes with her hand.

"What that means, I don't know,"

he said quietly. "Maybe they were following us, maybe not."

"If they weren't?"

"Then nothing is changed, and we go on to Gumsa, as planned."

"But?"

"If they *were* after us, then even more reason for being very careful, when we get there" — he gestured in the direction of the radar-station — "look the place over, before we go in."

"Why don't we give Gumsa a miss altogether?" she asked. "Go round, and press on regardless? We've probably enough petrol as it is." All at once she knew this was the right thing to do; intuitively and without question, *knew it.*

He thought it over, but shook his head. Said finally, "Maybe, but we need other things as well — water, especially water. Without more water we could be in terrible trouble, later on."

She made a face, but, eventually,

accepted it. Said, "You really think there may be a few Brits still left there?"

"Unlikely," he admitted. "But we have to go in and take a look, I think."

★ ★ ★

They had a good day, a lovely languorous sort of day, in the narrow gully they had found. A happy loving sort of day in which for long periods they managed to forget the world outside, and concentrate on themselves, their physical craving for one another, and their thoughts. That they might not be doing the right thing, by waiting for the night and then reconnoitring Gumsa on foot — thereby wasting valuable time to no purpose, even if there were no other, graver, risks involved — of course occurred to them, of course worried them, but once the decision to do that had been taken, by Andersen, she did not refer to it again.

They slept much, in the shade he rigged up at the back of the jeep; kept watch from time to time, but saw nothing; ate and drank, the last of his whisky, and generally recovered their forces, both physical and emotional. By the end of that day, hot though it had been, they didn't really care what happened to them from that time on: they had had some wonderful times together and could not but believe that there would be many more . . .

After nightfall they set out, dressed European again for ease of getting about, in jeans, shirts, sneakers. Took nothing with them but a canteen of water and a torch. The night cool, starlit, with a little wind, and they made good time, making first for the trail by which they had reached the high ground and, after finding it, turning north. As they walked along, not hurrying, using their torch occasionally to light their way, a big aircraft — an airliner almost certainly — crossed the night sky many thousands of feet above their heads, leading lights flashing, and they looked up, watched it disappear in time, but did not speak of it. After three quarters of an hour the lights of Gumsa appeared and, at Andersen's suggestion, they left the trail and circled a little to approach one of the gates from the side; did not use the torch at all from that point on.

Gumsa: within its perimeter of wire few lights lit, many fewer, surely, than would have normally been the case during the early hours of darkness had the site been fully staffed and functioning: there was the odd arc-light here and there, another over the gate they were approaching, and lights on in what might be a couple of barrack-blocks some distance off; nothing else, and no lights atop the tall masts, the foot of one of which they could just make out, away to their left. Not a soul to be seen, anywhere, not a sound but the distant hum of a generator breaking the night silence, and the gate they were approaching wide-open.

He halted, and she halted with him, but really, for all their misgivings, there was nothing left to do now but go in, that was what they had come here for, and the dangers involved were known to them. On impulse he turned to her, and they embraced, held each other a moment; before turning to the gateway once more. Together they went in, openly, hand in hand, and when they were inside made for one of the two well-lit barrack-blocks, four-five hundred yards away, past other buildings, sheds, godowns, all unlit. It seemed to take an age to get there but still no one accosted them and they saw no sign of life. In front of the barrack-block they had selected was a vehicle-park: Andersen shone the torch over jeeps, four in number, all with the insignia of the Ministry of Communications upon them; then they went to the wall of the barrack-block and listened under one of the open windows, light from within pouring out above their heads.

Inside someone had a radio turned on, a music programme — light music in western style — and when it was ended, came an announcement, in English, by an announcer whose voice they knew well; from the BBC World Service, its reception here far better than it had ever been at Ayoun.

He smiled, put his arm about her shoulders, briefly, and then they went quickly to the entrance: double-doors of solid timber, up some steps. He tried the handles, but the doors were locked, so he rapped hard on the wood-surface with his knuckles. No one came. He knocked again, harder, careless of the noise.

Behind them, suddenly, there was movement: men. Without hurry they came out of the shadows from either side, and stood in a half-circle round the foot of the steps, keeping their distance but cutting off all avenues of escape. Shadowy figures, Arab, rifles gleaming in their hands, they stood motionless, waiting. Until a voice said, in English, "Come down slowly. Raise your hands. If you make no trouble, no harm will come to you."

They stood very still, hesitating — and then did as they were told.

14

MIDNIGHT, and the worst thing that had happened to her so far was the fact of their separation. The men who had taken them — Arabs, total strangers — hadn't treated them badly, merely forced them at gunpoint to enter the building; then taken them upstairs and incarcerated them: herself in a storeroom, he somewhere else. When they had done that, she had cried out, fought, tried to run, but they had only sneered, bundled her inside, and locked the door; paid no heed to the hammering on the door she had kept up for a while. Later, after she had given up making a racket, two men brought her food and water on a tray which they set down on the floor by a stack of duplicating paper. Half an hour after that the lights had gone out.

She felt diminished, afraid, half-alive, because he wasn't there: afraid for him, her imaginings not one whit tempered by the reasonable treatment she herself had received up till that time. Long since she had got herself together, telling herself that she could only take things as they came, but found that nearly impossible. She had never loved anyone before in the way she did Andersen, with absolute commitment, for better or worse, that was apparent to her now in these circumstances more than ever and gave to the events of this evening and night all the pre-requisites of tragedy. To go on living, without him — if they took him away, or killed him, and she never saw him again — would be a travesty of existence and she didn't want it. Didn't want it, never mind what they did or didn't do to her.

Because she knew, with total certainty, that these people, whoever they were, who had taken them, were inimical. Young men, every one, not city or town-dwellers but from the desert, their speech Bedu of the cadence and dialect to be encountered around Kamil and Ayoun, their build wiry and lithe, hair often long and skin-colour dark: that they were under orders, this also obvious, and meticulously carrying them out, no more, no less. This was, in essence, as much the cause of her fear as anything else, that soon enough their orders would *change*, following which anything might happen: they were hard men, disciplined, and gave her the strongest of feelings that whatever they might be told — or given leave — to do, they would do it, without scruple and without question. So that the mind which controlled them (from afar?) that was the key factor, and who knew what sort of mind that was, or what it intended, very soon, or in the long run.

She had seen them looking her over, particularly the two of them who had brought in her food, and it was not that they lacked all mercy and compassion, she suspected, but that, because she was in their power (and did not conform to their rules) she *thereby* forfeited all sympathy as a human being in their eyes. The age-old Arab failing, made that much more repellent by reason of her construction, so to say, the fact that she was unmistakably a woman. While they were with her, and for the first time in her life, it occurred to her that truly it might have been better had she grown up ugly or deformed. Except that, to them, that probably made little difference . . .

Early on, while the light had lasted, she had prepared herself a place to sit, among the stacks of paper, and sat there now, in the darkness, sleepless, waiting. A heavy steel surveyor's rule across her lap.

* * *

The night was long, and the next day longer. She was fed and watered; only once taken out of the little storeroom. In the middle of the morning three men came and took her downstairs and outside: tethered her, hands tied behind her back, to the bumper of a jeep, with sufficient slack in the rope which held her so that she could stand, walk about a little, take the air. She had an hour like that, during which she saw no one, and then they came and put her back in the storeroom again. With her captors, when she saw them, she tried everything she could think of to make contact with them, cajolery, tears, abuse: to no avail, they would not speak to her, about *anything*; handled her, when they had to, with the same ruthless efficiency that they had employed from the start. Until she gave up, as the day wore on; did no more than spend a little time shouting, when the spirit moved her: calling out to Andersen, in case he remained within earshot, to let him know where she was, and that she was all right; but got no reply of any kind, formed no idea of where he might be, still in the building or not — or of whether he was still alive or already dead.

So, to the second night, and for all her forethought on the subject, the smell of her own excrement beginning to pervade the air of her windowless room. To distract herself from her predicament she read a manufacturer's manual concerned with the maintenance of photocopiers and other equipment; then, when that did not hold her attention, set out to sketch, in pencil, from memory, the set-up as it had been at Ayoun, the mounds, the circle of kabins, the little hills close by where she had sunbathed every day. She could draw quickly and well, not to professional standards, but usefully enough to assist sometimes in her work, and her efforts, spurred on by nostalgia, passed the time, engrossed her sufficiently to give her mind a period of rest.

But she was doing nothing again,

merely sitting waiting, when they came for her, just before ten. Three men again at the door, telling her to come with them.

"Where?" she demanded.

No reply, merely, from the doorway, one of the men beckoning her out into the lighted passage beyond.

She shook her head and stayed seated: anything, however insignificant, to make things less easy for them.

The man who had beckoned came into the room and stood over her, looking down into her face. She eyed him, her hand gripping tightly the steel rule at her side. She had seen him several times before, he was no stranger, one of the two who had been her jailer from the beginning, in his early twenties perhaps, undeniably handsome, with a small near-white scar on his left cheek. On a previous occasion he had actually smiled once when she had cursed him, had treated her with fractionally less disdain than the others when overpowering her struggles. This time he leaned forward and spat in her face.

She groaned, gritting her teeth, and wiped the spittle from nose and cheek with the back of her hand. But otherwise remained very still. Suddenly everything was changed, she knew it, and tried desperately to prepare herself for the worst.

"Get up. Come with us," the young man said quietly, and she did as she was told, leaving her 'weapon' where it was.

They took her out into the passage and turned right, a way she had never been before. One man leading, the other two at her elbow either side, they marched her to the end of the passage, turned left, marched her again, to the end of the building, to an office in which three other men waited, one of them seated at a big desk. Before this desk her escort halted, and moved to one side, so that she stood alone.

The man facing her, leaning back watching her in a big swivel-chair, was forty years old or more, narrow-eyed, dark, one of the most wolfish-looking men she had ever seen: a lined clean-shaven face that gave nothing, sinewy hands that tormented a mizpah on the blotter before him, prodding, rearranging the beads continually like a miser telling his hoard. He wore a black robe with no trace of decoration, open at the neck, and on his head a small skullcap, shiny black satin, ornamented with a pattern of white flowers. Averting her eyes from his she became aware that the five other men in the room, two seated, three standing, were all as motionless as statues, waiting for their leader to speak.

All he said was, "Take off your clothes."

"No" — her voice steady enough.

"Do as you're told!" — the order harsh, grating. "Or my men will do it for you."

She looked up, breathing through her mouth; round at the faces of the other five: they watched her, just waiting for the word of command, and two of them were smiling. So the tableau remained, without further movement, for a quarter of a minute, until she said slowly, "If I do what you wish, you will not hurt us? You will let us go, afterwards, my husband and myself?"

The man behind the desk leaned forward, taking up and clutching his mizpah in one hand. He glared at her, apparently angry to the point of explosion, but all he said was, "God is generous, God is merciful — ",

"I must *know*!" she cried. "My husband — ." But too late: at a sign two men had her by the arms, from behind, and a third was before her. She fought, writhed, bit, but in two minutes it was all over and she huddled naked on the floor before the desk, sobbing, head bowed and her arms hugging her breasts, as the three men stood back.

"Now, get up," their leader said inexorably.

She shook her head. Again she was seized, lifted, and forced to stand before the desk. Tears of helplessness, rejection, in her eyes, blinding her, and she let her body go limp so that they had to hold her up. In his chair the leader — his name apparently 'Tariki' — was talking again, saying something about how lucky she was. And she could not understand his words, but suddenly looked up, struggling again, and reviled him, calling him all the filthy names she knew, in the Arabic of her own country, Lebanon.

They took her out. Made her walk before them along the passage, her skin cringing, her mind numb. She felt sick, had pain in her back and abdomen, down her left leg, and limped a little, but held her head up as best she could. What would happen now would happen, she thought, and tried (again) to prepare herself for it, both mentally and physically, as far as she knew how. Rape, the despoliation of her body, by strangers, it was a little thing, surely a little thing, if only there were not too much pain. She feared pain, to be torn, maimed — please not, only that, the rest she could bear, *must* bear, since it was only a little thing: the body, hers, which now belonged solely to Andersen, which she had meant to keep exclusively for him — oh hell, never mind.

They took her down the stairs — unswept, and gritty gravel hurting her feet as she descended — and then out, through the main doors, into the night. Walked her over to one of the parked jeeps and told her to get in the front seat. Uncomprehending, she did that, and a man got in either side of her. The driver inserted keys, switched on and drove off: headlights cutting twin swathes of brilliance across buildings and bungalows as he turned.

Eventually she found her voice. "Where are we going?"

"Outside, to the desert," the driver said.

She didn't say anything more, thinking that, with these men, it was entirely fitting that what was going to happen

209

should happen somewhere in the sands which were their element, in the dark. At least, out there, it should not take long, that was something, and she might not see their faces, but that they were going outside meant, almost certainly, that they intended to kill her, afterwards. She stiffened in her seat and got herself together, finally, by sheer willpower, shivering with the effort. To run, at some stage, to be ready to run, as soon as the vehicle stopped, from that moment on: she had no hope of fighting them but must be ready to run. They would come after her, but surely, in the dark, there was some chance that she might get clear away, and thus, at least temporarily, save her life.

Four miles they drove, approximately that, in a northerly direction by the stars, across an empty landscape of high desert, rock and shallow ravines. Then, after a word with the man in the back, the driver drew the vehicle to a halt. The man beside her, on the passenger side, got out, held the door open for her, and she slipped across the seat — and as soon as her feet touched the sand took off, running as fast as she could into the darkness.

They let her go. The man who had been beside her got in again, and after a moment or two the driver restarted the engine, turned the jeep, and drove off, back in the direction they had come.

15

SHE ran until she could run no more. Then pitched forward on her knees in the sand, supporting herself on her hands, gasping for breath. When she thought about it, later, she could not understand how she had managed to run so far without stumbling, falling, but that was what happened, she neither tripped nor fell, in the event. After a while she lay down, on her back, arms thrown wide, and stared up at the stars.

In the darkness, left, she heard someone call her name; call it again, "Lina! Lina, are you there?" in a strident whisper, but did not answer for a few moments, unable to credit her senses, thinking that she must be hearing things. Then sat up with a jerk, and cried out, still fearfully. "Here! Here I am."

He found her then, Andersen, and crouched, gathering her to him: held her to him with all his strength, murmuring endearments — to which she gave him her sobbing replies and asked how he was — questioning her, caressing her, as she did him, the tears they shed of joy, relief and bewilderment. At length he breathed, "I've been waiting, half an hour. They said you'd come but I didn't believe them."

She murmured, "But why? I don't understand. Why this?"

Naked, as she was, he held her away from him, the shadow of his head and dark silhouette against the stars. Said only, "I don't know." Then, "They left us a canteen of water. Would you like some?"

"Please."

"Come," he said. "I've found a place, over there, out of the wind. It'll be less cold."

"I'm not cold," she said.

In the morning, a shamal was blowing, thick biting dust howling eerily across the face of the high plateau, and they kept down, huddled together in their little gully, praying that it would not last long. It was there, and while the shamal was still at its height, that the children found them: a little boy, a little girl, with cloths across their faces, they appeared suddenly together like apparitions through the streaming dust-storm and halted a yard or two away, shoulder to shoulder: the boy in shorts and shirt, the girl in shirt and denims. Lina saw them first, over Andersen's bowed back, and sat up, ducking her head into the wind and beckoning the children to her: European kids, neither more than ten years old. They came quickly and crouched down beside her, then lay down between the two adults, faces hidden, sheltering from the storm. Wordlessly, over their heads, she stared at Andersen; then lay down again, covering the children as best she could with her body, lowering her head until it was close to theirs. Feeling Andersen's arm come down across her shoulders as he gathered the three of them to him.

In half an hour the shamal blew itself out and the dust settled so that the sun shone through. For the two adults the pressing need now was to find shelter of some kind, clothing to cover their nakedness, or they would burn, dehydrate, in a few hours. Their curiosity and amazement at the advent of the children had to be satisfied, however, at least in part, before they did anything else. That the two kids had been alone out here in the wilderness, if that was the case, had to be explained. Heaven knew, but perhaps they were not alone.

The little boy was called 'Mike', and the little girl 'Tikka'. Through the dust which masked his features the boy had a bright earnest little face, and he did most of the talking while the girl sat shyly by, watching the two adults closely with bemused enquiring eyes. The boy said that Mummy and Daddy were 'over there' — he pointed somewhere to the north — but that they had had an accident, they didn't speak any more, and were 'very sick'. Quietly, probing further as he gave them water to drink, Andersen got from the boy a few more details, the young piping voice telling of a jeep that had overturned, and caught fire, of men who had visited them, maybe three days ago, Arabs, and of one man who had returned, the day before, a kind man who had brought water and told them that soon 'other people' would come and not to move from where they were.

"Is it far?" Lina asked, "to where the accident happened?" She was kneeling now, her back to the sun, and had the little girl in the crook of her arm, to shelter her and give her the human contact which was probably her greatest need. For the moment the little girl sat very still, looking up, studying Lina's face.

"Not far," the boy said. Then, eagerly, "I'll take you there, if you like — ?"

"No! Please, I don't want to see them again," the little girl whispered, and turning, hid her face between Lina's breasts.

"I'll go," Andersen said immediately, and he and the boy got to their feet together. To Lina he said, "You two, just stay here. We'll be back as soon as we can."

As they went off she heard the little boy ask suddenly, "Why haven't you got any clothes on?" — and Andersen's matter-of-fact reply, after a moment, "We lost them, in the night."

"I lose a lot of things too," the boy said. "People are always telling me."

As soon as the 'men' were out of sight, the little girl relaxed, smiling to herself, and shortly afterward left Lina's side and began to draw, with her forefinger and with great concentration, the face of a pig in the dust.

* * *

'Mummy' and 'Daddy' were both dead, of course, their bodies stretched out on the sand beside the gutted jeep and covered with flies. What was left of the jeep lay on its side at the foot of a steep 'wall' of sand and rock perhaps twenty feet in height and, as the little boy explained, when it had gone over, he and his sister, who had been in the back, had been thrown clear and — to Andersen almost miraculously — had survived without injury. Also thrown clear with them had been suitcases of clothes and other personal possessions, cans of water and petrol, a big cooler-box of food, but these had been plundered systematically by the Arabs who had found them and there was little left.

When he had made a quick inspection of what there was to see, Andersen sat the boy down in the shade of the rock-wall upwind from the two corpses and questioned him further. Where had they all been going?

To the sea, the boy said. Everyone had been very excited, they had packed quickly, at Gumsa, and had left there in the dark, three-four days ago. Many people, all their friends, six or seven jeeps there had been full of people; but their jeep had been the last to leave, some time after the others, because Daddy had been 'in charge'. When the accident happened they had been travelling fast, to catch up with the rest.

Andersen thought he saw how it must have been: the anxiety among the adults, the sudden decisions, the hurried preparations for departure, and then the flight itself. In the rush to get away the absence of 'Daddy' and his family not noticed for a while, perhaps for several hours, until everyone else had reached the place where they had agreed to spend the night. And even if someone had been sent back to look for them, after that, the chances of finding them, in the night, and once the jeep had burned itself out, not great. Sad, but at such times such things happened.

He told the boy to stay where he was, in the shade, and went over to the jeep again, to make a really thorough examination this time of all that was left. Thinking that they should hurry now, take every single thing that could be of any possible use to them, and then get on their way, before 'the Arabs' came back. That they would come back he felt certain: that was why, partly anyway, he and Lina had been released in the night, to find and look after these children. Back there at Gumsa someone had taken pity, in a callous sort of way, and did not want the two kids' deaths on his conscience. Allah Kerim, you might say. So they would come back, to check if the kids were still around, or not, and would probably do it before the end of the day.

Sickened, his hands clumsy and shaking, he stripped the dead bodies, which had hardly been touched; found, like manna from heaven, a useful-looking clasp-knife in the pockets of the man's slacks, but no wallet or other means of identification. He dressed in the man's things, never mind the smell and bloodstains, it had to be done, only the shoes would not fit him at all and he threw them aside. He made a pile of the woman's things for Lina, then turned his attention to what was left in the two broken suitcases. Clothes for the children in plenty — no one had seen much use for those — a couple of picture-books, files of paper, mostly technical, to do with 'Daddy's' job, but among them several maps; little else. Everything else had been carried off, but everything. He put clothes, including those for Lina, and the maps, into the better of the two suitcases, left it open while he went to look at the cooler-box, what remained of it, and the several metal and plastic containers nearby.

While he was doing so the little boy

called out and started over, to help, and was told, too roughly, to keep his distance.

One good container, half-full of water, the rest were damaged, empty; in the cooler-box foetid greens, rotting meat and polluted bread, but also two cans of cheese and another of Australian butter which, being Muslim, those who had visited this place after the accident had been chary of. He cleaned these off in his hands and then wrapped them in one of the boy's shirts and put them with the other things in the case. Then signalled to the boy that they were on their way.

16

FOR three nights they marched — hid up, finding what shelter they could for themselves during the day — until they reached the edge of the plateau. From there, on the morning of the fourth day, they could actually see the sea, fifty miles off, four-five days' march, downhill most of the way, if all went well. They still had a good chance, *if* all went well, of reaching the coast in time. Never mind that the other Brits from Gumsa had, in all probability, reached Ras Abu Khim and been picked up days before, the navy or whoever else it might be who had come for them would still hang about for some time yet in case Mike and Tikka's parents — perhaps others as well? — made it to the rendezvous. They would not simply up anchor and abandon any latecomers, they could not do that, surely, for a while yet.

So, that morning, with the distant sea in view and the saw-toothed ranges at their feet, their mood, for a while, was one of renewed hope: Lina and Andersen smiled wearily at one another and touched hands; Andersen hoisted the little boy onto his shoulders, from which point of vantage he keened and shouted, pointing and firing questions, until suddenly and without warning he sobered, began rubbing his eyes, and shed a few tears.

Because, truly, their situation was desperate: they had eaten the last of their food the evening before, had very little water, and Andersen's feet — though on the march he had wrapped them in rags, tied on hand-made soles to their soles — were in a frightful state, cut, blistered and beginning to fester. More than that, the little girl was ill, had terrible stomach-pains and diarrhoea, and had few reserves left —

So, he would carry her, Andersen said, both she and his feet could (and must) last another few days. There was a village not many miles distant, a little way down from the plateau, so their maps told them, called Mudhair: he would get into that village, this coming night, and steal water, food and anything else that might be of use to them that he could find. Then they would press on . . .

They had made their way to the shade of some rocks; sat down now to rest for a few minutes. A yard or two away the little boy crouched dejectedly, staring at something in the dust; at Lina's side the little girl lay comatose, filthy, already emaciated. Eventually, when Andersen had finished speaking, Lina looked up, not at him but into the distance, and said simply, "No, we can't do it like that."

"Why not?" he demanded.

"Because, if we do, this one will die," she said. She looked down again at the little girl and, briefly, caressed her head.

"You think she may be that bad?"

"It could *get* that bad, if something isn't done, very soon."

He nearly said "So what?", but managed to hold the words back. That, in the last three days, since finding them, Lina had become very attached to these children, in a much deeper way than he, he knew. He loved her for it, but resented it as well, try hard as he might not to, the fact that in some curious natural way that he did not want to understand she, through her closeness to these strays, had to some extent left him. It wasn't so really, he told himself, at least he hoped not, but nevertheless the feeling he had was too insistent to be denied. Still quietly, he said, "Maybe there's some sort of dispensary at the village. I shouldn't think so, but it's possible. Maybe I can find medicines for her."

"Not good enough." Her voice adamant but her eyes half-pleading with him and compassionate as well. "She needs rest as well as attention, for a few days, and *so do you*. You cannot go on like you are."

"Oh yes I can," he said, "and I damn well will."

She shrugged. Said only, without undue emphasis, "Then you'll have to go on by yourself."

He shook his head, made a big effort to calm the anger rising within him, and said throatily, reasonably, "You don't know these villages, up here in the mountains. They're very poor, very primitive — "

"Nevertheless," she interrupted, "I shall go, tonight, without you if necessary, and throw myself and these kids on the villagers' mercy. Beg, for food and somewhere to rest up, for a day or two."

"We're being *followed*," he persisted. "There isn't *time*. If we're going to make it to the coast."

"There has to be time," she said. "And as to being followed, with the idea of recapturing us, I don't think so. We're being 'watched', that's all."

227

"Why?" he asked curiously. Then nodded. "I'm inclined to agree with you, we're being watched, only. But why?"

"Perhaps it is only we ourselves who *think* we're being 'hounded'," she said. "'He', whoever he is, wants us to think that, but we're not really being hounded at all."

"If so, I don't understand," he said. "The whole thing's meaningless to me."

"Our own fears, our own ambitions," she said wearily. "Perhaps for the time being they are our worst enemies." She sighed, and then concluded, "Anyway, He can always finish us off when he wants to, can't he — or in the end?"

★ ★ ★

The village was built of mud-brick and woven matting and in all contained not more than twenty dwellings apart from a rudimentary mosque. It was perched on a narrow ridge over a chasm and reached by a winding path which began among stunted palm-trees and some wretched patches of cultivation. It was very old, the last hiding-place, perhaps, long ago, of a decimated tribe whose members' reputations had been so vile as to preclude their remaining in more civilised parts, and there were many signs of its once having been considerably bigger, many buildings here and there in total disrepair and returning to dust. Andersen, on sight of it, from a distance and in late afternoon, was more convinced than ever that they should give it a wide berth, but she could not be persuaded, so they went on.

As slowly, painfully, they climbed the path below the outlying walls they met their first villagers: grim bearded men in belted black thobes with blunderbusses in their hands. They appeared as if out of the ground and the straggling bush either side of the trail, and stood in a line across it, tall, very lean, very still, waiting for them to climb higher and approach. Carrying the little girl in his arms he halted some three yards from them, raised his eyes to the savage faces above, and allowed Lina, who had the little boy by the hand, time to come up beside him, before speaking. "Misa-il-kheer. The child is sick. We are travellers and need help." He winced, kept his voice low, but did not beg.

Silence. Above them the six men remained motionless, looking down at them; then two or three exchanged glances. One said, in a dialect barely recognisable as Arabic, "From whence you come?"

Andersen jerked his head. "From back there. Many miles. From Kamil" — but he thought that they neither understood him nor knew the place; it was too far, a long way beyond their ken.

"Faranji?"

"Yes." He nodded. "Faranji." That they were foreigners might or might not help, that remained to be seen, but to vouchsafe anything but the truth, at

230

this stage, was surely inadvisable.

Suddenly, without word of command, the men were coming down the slope, and surrounded them. Their leader, if he was their leader, stood at Andersen's side, staring at him intently, glancing at the girl-child in his arms, looking up once again into his eyes. Then the man smiled, revealing rotten teeth, and held out his hand. "Welcome" — a harsh spitting voice — "welcome." He nodded several times. "The village" — a gesture — "you can go."

Retaining his hold on the little girl, Andersen managed to shake the hand offered him. Said, "May God reward you," and so began his ascent, gritting his teeth against the pain in his crippled feet. Behind him he heard the little boy pipe up, "Are they Bedu? Shall we stay here? Will they give us food?" — and Lina's low reply, "Hush now, darling, when we get there we'll see. Let's just get there first." Andersen climbed on, while four of the mountain men accompanied them and two others detached themselves and ran up the path ahead, fleet-footed as gazelle, to prepare their reception. In the end they came to level ground, and stood panting, waiting, nearly spent. Andersen hugged the little girl to his chest and in her drowsy state the little one put her hands round his neck. She murmured something, coughed, choked, and then lay still against him.

They were in an alleyway between mud walls, shadowy, sandy underfoot. And suddenly there were many people at the end of the alley, staring at them, hanging back, calling out, pointing: women, young children, a few old men. At Andersen's side the bad-toothed man waved his arms, shouting, "Ruh! Ruh!" and the villagers vanished as quickly as they had appeared.

* * *

For three nights and days they remained in almost total seclusion, within the small walled compound of the house to which they were led that first evening: a tiny place of two rooms, its only windows two square holes at head-height in the adobe walls which looked out onto a yard at the back. There were roughly-woven mats upon the floor, pallets for sleeping on of sacking filled with palm-fibre but no other furniture of any kind. But at least the house and its roof were both in reasonable repair, the floor was clean-swept and out back there was a lean-to over a hole in the ground which served as an adequate latrine. That first evening, after a brief look round, they collapsed wearily, their minds alternately filled with gratitude, hope and trepidation, and prayed that very soon something in the way of sustenance might be brought to them.

For they were locked in: the heavy wooden door had been closed and barred behind them on entry and when they listened they could hear the shuffling of feet, the occasional low remark, made by two guards posted outside. Quite quickly darkness fell and all that they were left with was the sound of their own breathing, the small movements they made on the pallets on which they lay. Outside, the village seemed unnaturally silent. After a time Andersen crawled to the door and tried to converse with the men outside.

"We need water, food. We have none with us and all our water is gone."

"Patience." A low gruff voice in reply. "All is being prepared."

"It will come soon?"

"Insha'Allah."

"Please God, soon."

Silence again then and, after a while, Andersen returned to his place. His throat was clogged, thick with thirst by this time, and his gums and lips were cracked and swollen — the others in as wretched a state as he, nothing was more certain, the little girl moaning — yet to try to force matters, give way to his mounting bitterness, and anxiety, and fear, start throwing his weight about: it was too early to do that. Who knew what these people intended, perhaps they themselves had not made up their minds, and meanwhile the four of them were totally at their mercy.

Beside Lina the little girl began to cough weakly, and Lina crooned to her and shortly took her out back. While they were away the little boy, Mike, crawled over to him, felt for his hand; then leaned against his side as Andersen put an arm around his shoulders. For a long time they sat like that, in the darkness, without speaking.

Actually very little time elapsed, perhaps twenty minutes, before all at once there was movement outside, beyond the door: several people, heavy breathing, and through a crack in the door Andersen could see the yellow light of one or more lanterns. There was muted conversation, wholly incomprehensible, the sound of weighty objects being placed upon the ground, and then after a while the swishing sound of sandals moving away.

A few seconds longer, and then the door was unbarred, pulled back by unseen hands, and left open. Outside, on the ground, with a single hurricane lantern illuminating it, was a feast: a big coppered tray piled high with rice, big pieces of roasted chicken embedded in it; beside that other dishes of boiled pumpkin, cucumbers and brinjal; a big enamel jug of goatsmilk; calabashes of water to one side and a kettle of tea, with glasses from which to drink. In the night air the aroma of spicy wholesome food was like the breath of Heaven, and Andersen led Lina and the boy quickly outside, sat down cross-legged by the big tray, motioning to the others to sit down as he was doing opposite him. First, their hands trembling, they relieved their thirst; then they ate. There was far and away too much, as custom demanded, of this, surely the very best that the village could provide, a repast of a kind and in such quantity as villagers like these might themselves know once or twice a year, at most. They ate, drank, until they could eat and drink no more, and all the time saw no one, no one at all, in the darkness that surrounded them, though they were aware there were people out there, beyond the circle of light, watching them.

When they had finished Andersen looked round and spoke words of thanks into the darkness. They were not necessary, he knew, but he had to do it. Then, with the lamp, water, and a single dish of food for the little girl, such as she might be able to eat, they went back inside, leaving the door open behind them.

Shortly it was closed, barred again, and people could be heard removing dishes and uneaten food. A little while after that the man of the diseased teeth announced his presence outside and the door was reopened. He had an old woman, her face hidden, in black, with him. She went quickly to where the little girl lay, on one of the pallets, and studied her condition while Andersen held the light for her. After that she examined Andersen's feet. Then she went out again, the village Headman following her, and the door was closed once more. Not for long, for in a few minutes she returned — again with the man, whose name was Yusef, in attendance — both this time carrying small calabashes and a steaming kettle of boiling water, clean cloths. The old woman knelt down beside the little girl, mixed something in a bowl and made her drink, cleaned her, and then covered her with a blanket. After which she doctored Andersen's feet with a concoction of oil and aromatic herbs and bound them round loosely with strips of cloth.

17

AT Mudhair a different relationship had grown up between Andersen and the little boy, Mike: he had begun to notice and respond to the loneliness he sensed in the boy's eyes and to feel protective towards him. On the boy's part he seemed anxious to be with Andersen all the time, help him, take part and contribute to anything which the man felt it necessary to do. He, the boy, suddenly seemed also more mature, the puppyish ways of his early days with them vanishing without trace in the course of that short period of incarceration, and Andersen began to like him. He was a good kid, who perhaps at home had been badly spoilt, but now, in totally different circumstances, put all that quickly behind him.

So, on the march from Mudhair to the next village, Askar — much bigger, by repute, much richer and more prosperous — it was often 'the men' who led the way, and 'the girls' who brought up the rear; the little girl, now 'Patricia' and no longer the babyish 'Tikka', almost completely recovered, thinner in face and body, but able and determined enough to keep up.

Nevertheless Lina made sure that they didn't push on too fast and so overtax the children's strength, once having a stand-up row with Andersen when, one afternoon, he wanted to go on just that much longer, to 'that rise over there' and could not easily be persuaded that the other three had had enough for the day: a row that did not stay with them for long, was soon made up after they had all found a place to camp and rested, but which shocked them and made them pensive for a while.

This happened on the second day out from Mudhair and they expected

240

to reach Askar by mid-morning the day following: in two days nearly twenty miles had been covered and the terrain through which they passed was becoming easier, less mountainous all the time: the rocky gorges and narrow defiles of the heights giving way imperceptibly to less broken country, better (if still sparsely) watered, and showed signs occasionally of the presence of nomads and herdsmen. Not that they had met up with a living soul this far, and hoped that — some miles distant from the main 'road' down from the heights as they were — they could avoid doing so. Such people, Andersen said, might prove friendly but also might not, you could never tell and, this second day, he had insisted that they maintain a sharp look-out at all times.

But they were not being 'followed' any more, of that much they were fairly certain. Why, they didn't know, and could only pray that it might be because those who had been pursuing them had given up and gone home.

A faint hope, in fact, they believed, because those people back at Gumsa, Tariki and the man behind him, were not the sort to give up, or change their minds, and they were still, and would always remain, within His territory. Yet, who knew, other factors might conceivably have intervened.

In any case, that evening of the second day, they were much too weary to care. For the moment they were 'safe', and that was enough, in a narrow ravine shaded by a stand of acacia trees, in a small clearing between boulders among which grew tussocks of spiky reed-grass which betokened the presence of underground water beneath. They had eaten their fill of rice and beans with which the villagers of Mudhair, that remote and otherwise friendless place, had provided them, and now lay stretched out on the ground, arms up shading their eyes, as they digested, rested and took stock. Beside Lina lay the little girl, at Andersen's shoulder the boy, and each pair 'conversed' sometimes, at others and for long periods held their peace. Eventually Lina began telling the little one a story, a nineteenth century Arabian Nights fantasy that she made up as she went along, of a Lebanese prince and an icon of great price, of a poor girl of great beauty who found it but did not recognise her treasure for what it was, of a dramatic rescue, and love ever after — and while she spoke, spinning out her tale, the little girl watched her entranced and gradually the two men began to listen also, drinking in every word as though it were the greatest story ever told.

But while she drew them to her in this way Lina was thinking of the little one at her side, assessing, knowing, judging her: loving her and trying to read her fortune. What sort of kid was she and what chance did she have? What chance could they give her, because she was 'theirs' now and otherwise alone in the world. For the time being, perhaps for always, alone. There was a restlessness, a new maturity, growing in the little one, as she recovered her strength, which Lina found intensely moving, and very soon, she knew, the kind of story she was presently relating would become meaningless to her, at best a bit of a joke.

When she had finished the little girl sighed, rolled over onto her side, and within seconds fell asleep, her head pillowed on her arm. Lina sat up, ran her fingers through her hair, and found Andersen watching her. She got to her feet, turned to him; and he rose immediately, slapped some of the dust from his clothes, and spoke quietly to the little boy.

"You stay here, Michael, don't move, eh? Lina and I are going for a walk, we won't be long. You stay with Patricia, and don't make a noise, OK? Have some more water if you want to."

The boy looked up, blinking. "Can't I come with you?"

"No, not this time. Look, why don't

you collect some sticks, so that later we can make a fire, over there?" He pointed out a spread of rocks under one of the nearby trees. The night before, in the open, had been bitter cold and truly to make a fire, in a secluded spot such as this, didn't seem too much of a risk.

"All right," the boy said grudgingly, but then his face brightened and he got up and started searching around . . .

The two of them moved away, down the ravine, picking their way between and occasionally clambering over outcrops of naked rock. Came to a further fault in the land and descended again into a sandy open space probably hollowed out and cleared by water during the rains of millions of years. Here, as she joined him, Andersen held her by the shoulders and studied her face, held her to him, and then looked at her, really looked her over, again. Her face was haggard, shiny with sweat, streaked with dust and grime, and her hair a wilderness; at the corner of her mouth was a nasty weeping sore and her lips were badly chapped; she was thin, savagely thin, and her clothes, a tattered shirt and trousers, hung loosely from her shoulders and hips, dusty and hard-used like the rest of her. He shook his head, a lump rising in his throat, because he loved her so much and there had been no time, no thought, no physical strength, to tell her, for too long.

She smiled, facing him unflinchingly. Said, "You're no oil-painting, yourself." Seeing how these last days had changed him, hardened him, hurt him, lost him to her for a brief but vital period of their lives. Knowing that they were different people now, very different from the two who had made their decisions that day at Ayoun, both bound together by ties far stronger than those then pledged but at the same time weary of their lot and their struggles, and therefore, in some indefinable way, of one another. That she would love him always she knew — was ready to love him physically, in a few seconds time, if that was what he wanted — but never again with the same abandonment and joy that had once been hers. So sad, so natural, she supposed, but that was life. Perhaps she understood that better than he. After watching him a moment longer she reached out, came to him, ducking her head in under his chin, and held him fiercely to her, using her hips and belly erotically to stimulate and caress his manhood.

But after hugging her strongly in return he disengaged himself gently and turned away. Stood a moment, his jaw set, his eyes looking off into the distance unblinking; and then turned to her again, put an arm around her shoulders and guided her, a few steps, to a sloping bank of sand, where he sat down and, taking her hand, drew her down beside him. Her shoulder touching his she might have wept then, nearly did, but held back her tears, mastered the weakness in her limbs, by an effort of will. Determined, whatever it might cost her, to hang on, hold them together, take this changed relationship that was now theirs and make it work for them, not against.

For ten minutes they sat together, in silence: both of them thought to speak on several occasions, but then declined to break the spell. A different closeness upon them, lacking all illusion: probably between them there *was* nothing further to say, they realised that, but held hands tightly, at one stage, by way of defiance.

But after ten minutes or so returned to the world about them, and got to their feet. He spoke her name; she spoke his; it was a little like taking leave of one another, only not that. In both of them were the first stirrings of a renewed happiness. They embraced once more; then, because they were both emotionally exhausted and a little shy of one another, set out to return to camp.

On arrival there found no trace of either of the children. They had gone — where? They called, searched everywhere in the vicinity of camp, found the children's footprints in sand above the ravine, where the land rose across a broad stony plain to the next line of hills; but lost their trail again immediately. Dusk was upon them, barely twenty minutes of daylight left.

* * *

They 'wasted' two whole days searching for the children: days that should have taken them on, well past Askar, to within striking distance of the sea. During those days Andersen cursed their ill-fortune many times; cursed himself for not being stricter with the boy when he had had the chance; in his despair turned on Lina and blamed her as well, unjustly, for her lack of care in not instilling a sufficient sense of 'responsibility' into their charges. Other times he was tempted, sorely, to abandon the kids to their fate, and go, but knew, and in some part resented, that his woman would never consent to that, not for many days at least. Because the kids might be lying up somewhere, hurt, because they might, just possibly, have been abducted, and it was their duty to succour and find them if it was humanly possible to do so. So they continued looking for them, widening the circle of their search every time they set out, returning to camp in the ravine at two–three hour intervals, to rest, and eat, their lack of success as time passed rendering them increasingly bitter and estranged.

Eventually Andersen came upon them, nearly five miles from camp, in a stretch of broken country, the scene of some ancient cataclysm, amid low descending ranges. They were not hurt, nor had they been abducted, they had simply got lost, that first evening, and in their efforts to return 'home' had succeeded only in putting more distance between themselves and their objective. Andersen was so relieved to see them, in good health and unharmed, that he could not for the life of him be harsh with them, as he had intended, could not bring himself to give the boy the good hiding which he believed must surely be deserved. Merely hugged the two of them to him, when they ran up, caressed them and listened to their stories, as they started off to return to camp.

They had spent the first night in the open, it had been cold and frightening, but the next morning, while looking for a way back, calling all the time, they had found water, a spring. So they had gone on eagerly, in the direction they supposed the camp to be, until they had come to an abandoned Bedu encampment. There, within a leaning hut of palm-fronds and sacking, they had rested and finally fallen asleep. When they awoke had gone looking for food and water. And by a miracle had found both: a rock-pool, not too stagnant, and beside it a tiny patch of soil, once cultivated, in which a few small pumpkins, some nearly ripe, were left. So, sensibly enough, they had decided to stay within reach of their little 'oasis' and to continue their search for camp from there, which was what they had done, without success, all through the second day. Only by the third night had they become frightened again, one keeping watch beside their pool, in the approved manner, while the other slept: thinking of snakes and wolves and starting up at every sound. But luckily, not far along into the third morning, had heard Andersen's voice, calling their names, in the distance.

He laid down the law then, sternly, as they walked along, their hands in his. They *must* keep together, all of them, at all times, they *must not* stray off by themselves ever again. They weren't bairns any longer, they must use their *heads, think*, realise that anything that held them up, in this journey of theirs to the sea, could mean sorrow and death to them all. They had acted like halfwits, in going off on their own without letting anyone know, thereby causing Lina and himself great anxiety, and had better grow up, now, very fast. And the pair of them apologised, contrite, looking down before straightening their shoulders and stating categorically that from now on he could count on them, they had learnt their lesson, and so on.

When they reached the vicinity of camp, Lina ran out to meet them, fell on her knees to hug them to her and bury her face in their warmth and flesh, shaking her head and choking back tears.

18

WEARY though they all were — especially the two adults, on whom the last two days had taken their toll — they decided they had to set out again that day; they had lost too much time already and, besides, their food and water were almost gone. Which meant that, whatever the risks involved, they had to go into Askar now, and hope to find, among other things, some sort of vehicle — beg, borrow or steal it — and so get themselves *quickly* to the sea. There was still a fair chance, they believed, that the navy would be out there yet, off Ras Abu Khim, but they would be unlikely to be there much longer. In Askar too it was possible that they might obtain news, or listen in to a radio, and so find out what was happening in the country. Conceivably, just conceivably, the situation might have changed out of all recognition, for the better, and their troubles might be over. A forlorn hope that, but you never knew, it was a faint possibility that could not quite be ruled out.

Thus, it became a question of which of them should go into Askar and when: only one of them, meaning Andersen, which he insisted was the only sensible course, or all of them together, in a group? As they marched, down barren valleys and along sloping hillsides, in the general direction of the village, they talked it over. If he was to go in by himself — *surely* the safest course? — Andersen said, then he would go in at night, tonight; he knew, as well as anyone, the sort of layout he was likely to encounter in a small outback village, and later there would be a three-quarter moon.

But she wouldn't hear of it: quietly, firmly, she argued with him, saying that if he went in by himself, and was taken, what then? By themselves she and the young ones stood very little chance: either of 'rescuing' him or of making it on their own to the sea — still twenty, twenty-five miles distant. With the countryside roused and on the lookout for them, and himself held 'hostage', the thing wasn't on. They needed, *she* needed, him with them, she loved him, and they had made it thus far and against many odds *together*: let them continue, therefore, together, or not at all. Let them go into Askar, as they had done into Mudhair, openly, as a group, a family, and hope against hope that good fortune would be theirs, a second time.

He tried to reason with her, for a while, but then gave in. There were pros and cons, both ways, and the way she proposed might truly be the best course.

★ ★ ★

Around eight the next morning they sat together half way down a long slope of rocky hillside, and drank the last of their water. Below them lay the village, mud-walled houses, a mosque, surrounded by plantations of mature date-palms, citrus groves, and fields of alfalfa. To their right, some distance away and descending from the heights, was the main 'road', little more than a roughly graded track, which they had avoided for so long; and as they watched a jeep came into view, trailing its dust-cloud, disappeared, appeared again, as it made its way down towards the village. After a time the jeep disappeared once more among the trees; there was a pause, a minute or two, and then suddenly they saw it leave the village on the far side, heading for the coast.

Of course, by this hour, there were people down there, below them: men and boys working in the fields, women in black abeyas and strikingly patterned kangas, and they knew they had been spotted long since. No one, however, approached them, no one, as far as they could see, either stared in their direction or pointed them out to others. As if that they were out there beyond the confines of the village was of no importance or interest. Either that, or because they were expected and had been for some time. A thought that did little to make their day.

Yet there was no real alternative, now, to seeing what the village held in store for them, and soon enough Andersen made a move, got to his feet, turned and helped Lina to hers. Telling the children to stay close, they went down in single file, in silence, until gradually they reached level ground. They walked on, towards the first palm-trees gleaming in the early sunlight and the living-places they concealed. In the fields among which their path took them, sometimes surrounded by low walls of stone, people watched them go by but neither smiled nor greeted them. Until they were almost to the shelter of the trees, their trail leading them on into the shadows beneath, when men rose up to bar their way and stood waiting: half a dozen men. At their head the young man who had been one of their jailors at Gumsa, the one who, just prior to their release, had spat in Lina's face: handsome, dark-skinned, dressed today in tee-shirt and jeans. He came forward; held out his hand to each one of them in turn, Andersen first, then Lina, then the two children one after the other. So they shook hands, seeing the smile on the young man's face which did not reach his eyes. After that the young man made his dispositions: Andersen to go with so and so, the two children with Fulan, Lina with Mustafa and himself —

"We stay *together*!" Andersen said aggressively. But with little hope. He stepped back, glancing to right and left; ready — to do what? There was nothing to be done. He held out his hands, pleading now — "We're a *family*! We should remain together, for the children's sake."

But the young man only shook his head. Said quietly, "No."

"Why not?"

The young man shrugged. "Because life is full of sorrow, is it not?" he said seriously. "Because it is never as anyone of us may wish it to be."

"Words!" Andersen snapped.

"Only words," the young man agreed. "But they reveal a truth, I suppose, nevertheless."

19

NOW that it was all over — surely all over — reaction set in. As the young man led her through the village, along narrow alleyways between dun-coloured mud-walls, shadowy and dim under the trees, she could hardly walk and tears trickled down her cheeks. But after a while dried her eyes with the backs of her hands, and stumbled along, head down. Then all at once there were people, men, women and children lining the route, mostly silent, all staring, and she straightened, held her head up, and began to watch where they were leading her.

To a small compound on the far side of the village, eventually a small isolated house with two shuttered windows facing out over abandoned 'gardens', and a metal door, its hasp fastened by a big old-fashioned padlock. This the young man unlocked with a key he took from his pocket, pushed the door open, and then waved her inside.

She stood her ground and shook her head.

He came to her then, down the steps, and stood before her: looked expressionlessly into her eyes. Behind her she could feel the other man, the villager, very close. Suddenly the man behind her grabbed her by the arms and at the same time, quick as lightning, the young man lunged at her, one hand clawing at her face: forcing her head back, brutal fingers jabbing up into her nostrils. She shrieked, taken by surprise; tried to knee him, but he was out of reach; struggled, but the pain only became intense, unbearable — until she was whimpering, blubbering, and held herself still. He jerked her forward then, one finger up her nose; led her blind, witless, groaning, up the steps, through the doorway and into a darkened room, where he released her, as did the man behind her. She staggered, collapsed against the wall, her face in her hands, half conscious, half-hearing him say, "You are filthy — clean yourself up. There is food, so eat. I will come again, later." Then the outer door was slammed to and she was in semi-darkness.

★ ★ ★

He arrived a second time in the early afternoon, with him the same villager as before, a chunky ill-favoured individual with a cast in one eye. She was waiting for him out in the yard at the back of the house, a big 'splinter' of timber, which had obviously been left there by accident, like a dagger in her hand. All around her the high walls of the small compound, of concrete blocks topped by broken glass, hemmed her in and made escape impossible: she had tried, so hard, since first he had left her in that place, but all she had succeeded in doing was to exhaust herself and cut her hands badly.

He watched her from a few paces away and then came towards her, the villager circling right to take her from the side. She crouched, catlike, knowing it to be hopeless, but determined to make them pay, that whatever they wanted it should not happen easily, without a fight.

With cold-blooded unconcern he forced her to retreat, to the wall; then, as she struck at him, kicked her with all his strength in the stomach, doubling her up, all defences gone. Then the two of them beat her up, made her stand, beat her again, using fists, elbows, forearms; kicked her savagely when she fell; until she lay bleeding and semi-conscious at their feet. Then the young man bent down, lifted her in his arms and carried her back into the house, to the room in which there was a mattress on the floor. He laid her down gently, and then held her by the shoulders while the villager brought water, washed the blood off her face with a cloth, and gave her some of it to drink. When he saw that she was recovered a little and breathing without difficulty again, he got to his feet; stood looking down at her a few moments, and then he and the villager went away.

When he came again it was night, and the villager who accompanied him carried with him a big tray of food: rice, vegetables, meat. He found her still lying on her mattress, in pain, her face swollen and bruised, one eye closed. The villager set down the tray in the middle of the floor, went out again, to return with a carafe of water and glasses; then withdrew. Watching her the young man set his lantern down on the floor beside the tray, and sat down himself, cross-legged, to eat. He didn't hurry, made a considerable meal, but still, when he had finished, there was plenty left. After rinsing his hands he drank and lit a cigarette. Sat back and eventually said, "Come, why don't you eat? The food is good, and it is a shame to waste it."

"What do you want of me?" she asked, speaking with difficulty, not looking at him.

"I want you," he said. "When you are ready."

She turned her head further away and said nothing. After a while the young man got up and stretched, looking down at her. Said quietly, "In a few minutes a woman will come to you. Do not hurt or blame her because she is of no importance. She will help you, bring medicines if you need them, and stay with you tonight. You understand?"

When the young man had gone, she sat up carefully and after a time, when she thought she could manage it, got to her feet and went slowly out into the yard at the back. Breathing heavily through her mouth and holding her side from time to time she drew water from the cistern, stripped and dowsed herself down. Felt a little better after that and her headache not so crushing as before. Limped back into her room and when her body was dry put on a robe of heavy cotton which had been there with the mattress from the beginning. Then ate, as much as she could, to keep her strength up and because who knew when her next meal might come, choosing mostly rice and vegetables that she could swallow without chewing, washing the food down with plenty of water.

After ten minutes, and still no sign of the woman who was supposed to come, she began to realise that either the water or the food had been drugged. Cursed the young man then, railed against him in her mind — railed against her own helplessness and fear — until oblivion overtook her.

★ ★ ★

She woke with his naked body covering hers, as he caressed her preparatory to penetrating her. Hard male body that she thought at first was Andersen's and welcomed drowsily, until her pain returned and she remembered where she was and to whom these hands, this mouth, this body belonged, when she fought him with all her remaining strength, hitting out at him with her fists, trying to writhe out from under him. To no avail, she was much too weak, too sick, and he only laughed and held her easily, and in his own time took her, slowly, even gently, making sure that pleasure, of a kind, was hers as well as his.

As his climax approached, she heard him say between his teeth, "Habibti!" — you darling — "relax, that is all, enjoy, that is all, and I will give you a jeep, do you see? You shall have a jeep, you and your man, to get away. In time, I promise, that will be yours." After that she fought him no more, half-believing him, half not, crying and nearly spent, letting him do what he liked until he was satisfied.

20

THEY chained him, in place of a beast, to a massive 'wheel' which, by means of cogs, pulleys and ropes, drew water from a deep well: crippling hard labour, under constant threat of a rawhide lash. He stuck it for four hours, the first time, before passing out. They revived him and then let him rest, in the shade, for an hour, giving him water and something to eat, before setting him to work again. The young man from Gumsa, Seifuddin's man, came to join the crowd of onlookers from time to time, never saying a word; once took the whip himself and scourged him with it until the unoiled wooden axle of the wheel screamed in its sockets, the sweat poured from his naked body, and he was half-senseless with pain.

At dusk they released him. He

collapsed. Two men lifted him and carried him to an unlighted hovel nearby, where they threw him down. On the mud floor he straightened his body, rolled over and slept. His last thought: that they were setting out to work him to death. So let him die then. Let it be over. Soon.

The second day was worse than the first. He was weaker, his limbs stiff and shambling, his hands torn and nearly useless; his back lacerated, festering, a seething agony of pain. He sobbed, slobbered, when the lash bit into him, reopening old wounds, and passed out often. His wounds stank; clouds of flies hung over him and laid their eggs in his flesh; he could smell his own excrement on his body, and the reek of vomit rising from the circular path he trod out in the dust. Sometimes he thought of Lina, and the kids, but to think of them, and of what might be happening *to them*, was only additional torment — that he had led them to this, no one else — and *he* had just enough sense remaining not to let his mind dwell on their plight. His captors would only think their task so much the better performed, he suspected, if they drove him to madness.

Yet, strangely, as the day wore on, he grew a little stronger, clearer in the head, and the two youths who plied the whip in turn were given less excuse to practice their innate viciousness upon him. Not that they didn't go for him still, from time to time, when they felt so inclined (they had been carefully chosen, doubtless), they did, especially when the man from Gumsa was present. It was to *that one*, Andersen thought, that one particularly, that he hoped one day, and if he lasted long enough, to have the chance to pay back a little of what he owed.

Nevertheless by the second evening he was done, not far from death, he believed; he could not take another day, and his back was in an appalling state. In the empty room, in the hovel, in which they again incarcerated him once darkness fell, he passed out, for many hours, without touching the food and water left him. Woke only because there was light in the room, lamplight, movement and whispered conversation. Painfully, he sat up.

In the doorway stood a man, in thobe and sandals, but his face invisible in the shadows: the young man from Gumsa all the same, Andersen knew him. At his feet, squatting on the floor just within the room, a young girl, her kanga over her shoulders and masking the lower part of her face, her eyes narrow, and watching him with distaste. She had brought with her several small earthenware jars containing who knew what, and from them came a strong aroma of spices and herbs.

"Lie down and turn over," the young man said, from the doorway. "Aisha will doctor your back."

★ ★ ★

He got through the third day because he had begun again to trust in his great strength to pull him through, and because now he really *wanted* to survive: wanted to and had some hope. The young girl had apparently known her business because although she had inflicted terrible pain upon him and virtually left him for dead, the pain had quickly passed and his back had begun to feel as though, given time, it might possibly heal again. For the first time too since his ordeal had begun he had eaten well and kept it down, taken in sufficient water to keep dehydration at bay. Yet the third day was actually no easier than those that had gone before, they still lashed him, reopening old wounds, they still drove him until he dropped; the same ring of onlookers continued to watch him as though he were providing the spectacle of the year. But he could take it now, the work *seemed* easier, and he could begin to imagine a time, in the not too distant future, when he might attempt a break for freedom. When he did that, he promised himself, he would kill and kill again, with a weapon if he had one, with his bare hands if necessary, and thus assuage a little of the rage that by this time consumed his thoughts. Very likely it was this anger, at these people and their dreadful world, that kept him going that third day. He *despised* them now, every man-jack of them, and knew that he would never forget.

But he could not despise the young girl. Again she came to him during the night, the young man once more in attendance. As she ministered to him, and between bouts of near-unbearable pain, he watched her. She was perhaps sixteen, probably only recently married, and had a narrow chiselled face and long luminous eyes. Eyes that had lost the revulsion with which they had viewed him at the start and now mirrored only her compassion. She had lovely long-fingered hands and when she first touched him he could feel her fingers tremble, when she first hurt him she flinched, as though she were feeling something of his agony herself. Yet there was strength in those hands, and guiding them a mind both competent and determined, he realised, because when she really needed to hurt him, as she cleaned or applied dressings to his wounds, then she did not flinch, merely got on with her task, in silence, her whole being concentrated on what needed to be done.

When she was finished and was gone he felt, for a while, as though a great weight had been lifted from his mind.

* * *

On the fourth day the whips were still out, and the two youths with him, but the whips were never used. There was no need: he did the work they set him to do, hard, soul-destroying though it was, without too much suffering, and he was allowed, he thought, more frequent periods of rest than on previous days. Why, he had little idea, only guessing that something was going on behind the scenes that he didn't understand — either that or, just possibly, because since arriving in the village he had actually earned people's respect . . . They unchained him early, before the sun was quite down, allowed him to wash and slake his thirst at the well, and then gave him a cloth to tie round his waist and cover his nakedness. All this he took as it came, saying no word, merely doing what he was told, waiting, holding himself in check, counselling himself not to make his bid for freedom too soon, at all costs not to do that, until he was rested, until he had recouped his forces a little, or he would stand no chance.

Not long after they had taken him back to the hut which had become his night-time prison, the young girl, Aisha, came to him, bringing her jars of salves and unguents with her as usual, but this time alone. He allowed her to look at his back, and when she had finished, spoke to her for the first time. "It feels better. Will it heal?"

She had been kneeling beside him, and now sat back on her heels, eyeing him as he rolled onto his side to look up at her. She shook her head and said simply, "I don't know why, but I think yes, it will heal. You have been very lucky" — a quiet young-old voice as though there were a maturity in her far beyond her years.

"I'm deeply grateful to you," he said. "For all you've done."

"You have great courage," she murmured, and then looked away in embarrassment, before getting to her feet. She was very slim, quite tall, and also, it dawned on Andersen then, extraordinarily beautiful, in a natural, coltish sort of way.

"Will you stay with me a little while?" he asked, still looking up at her. "And talk?"

She nodded, but then made a face, a gesture. Said, "But not here. Come." She reached down a hand to him.

"There is food, and a better room, next door." She showed him a big key.

About the 'better room' she could only be right, he thought, as he got to his feet and stood swaying, for a few seconds, willing himself not to faint. Any other room had to be better than this one, reeking as it did of blood, and sweat, and excrement: his own.

★ ★ ★

After they had eaten he questioned her, and quietly, humbly, she told him the story of her life. She had been orphaned a long time ago, as a baby, at a time when sickness had carried off half the village, and had been taken in by distant relatives. These relatives, who had now moved away from the village, she didn't know where, had fed her, clothed her, but otherwise treated her, as soon as she was any use to them, as a skivvy: a body, female, without hope or prospects and without value. They had beaten her, often, given her enough to keep her alive (as custom demanded) but no love, no affection, no heritage, and when she was eleven had married her off to an old man of seventy-odd years whose fourth wife — and two others still living — she became. Again in that house she had been treated as a slave, had been 'forced' and defiled by a man whose sexual proclivities and mere presence made her shudder to remember, until finally he had grown tired of her and thrown her out on the street. That had been four, five years ago, a long time ago anyway, she didn't really recall how long ago it had been.

"And since then?" Andersen prompted her.

She was sitting opposite him, the tray of food, the pitcher of water pushed to one side, the light of the single lantern hanging from a roof-beam giving brilliance and shadow to her clean aquiline good-looks. But when she looked up, at him, he felt himself in the presence suddenly of a

279

different person, a girl yet, but savage, a predator, a terrible mixture of light and dark: her eyes like gleaming amber, but unseeing, looking inward, as though he wasn't there.

He shifted his position, startled, and sat back. Drew breath, but did not speak. Waited, quite still, for her to go on. Moved, very moved, and curious to know what more she might have to tell him.

"Since then," she said, after a time, "I have become — as you see me." She stood up in a single lithe movement, and let her kanga fall from her shoulders. She was dressed coolie-style, in middy-blouse and cloth tied low on her hips, to reveal the lovely lines of her narrow waist, the young perfection of her body. Watching him, smiling a little now, she raised her arms high above her head, and displayed herself to him: turning full circle until she faced him again. "Am I not beautiful?" she asked softly. "To you, as to other men?" She reached behind her, unpinned her hair, and tossed her head to allow it to fall loose over her shoulders and down her back.

"Very beautiful," he said.

"But I have let no man touch me!" she snapped, and sat down again. Continued to stare at him, and then went on, "Since that time, when there was that change in me, I have seen the look in men's eyes when I pass, I have seen them want, and scheme, and suffer. From time to time I have even listened to their offers, but in every case I have spurned them, one by one. There is an old woman who lives on the outskirts of the village, over there." She threw out her hand, pointing, as though she saw the place vividly in her mind. "I have lived with her, and for her, and learned from her the things that she knows, about herbs and medicines." She looked away, and added, "She has been very good to me, and I have loved her in return."

"But now?" Andersen asked quietly.

"Now?" the girl replied. Suddenly

she shook herself and laughed, really laughed, for the first time: a joyous youthful laugh, that once again caught him unprepared. "Now," she said simply, "I am a woman, and sometimes I want a man."

He stared at her without speaking.

"Sometimes I know," she went on, "that I can love a man properly, and give myself to him, in faith and trust. A certain kind of man, if I can find him."

"You will find him," he murmured. "I pray God that you will."

"Perhaps I have found him already."

He shook his head, watching her as she rose to her feet and came to him. Again she knelt beside him, then prostrated herself before him, her body trembling, her forehead to the ground. But said distinctly, "All I have is a little beauty, a little skill in healing. But also" — she sat back, and her face ravaged now, wet with tears — "but also much love, in here." She touched her breast with one hand. "Much love, waiting, to give."

"To me?" he asked, not looking at her. "Why?"

"Because you are strong," she said. "Because you have endured so much. Because you are a foreigner and not of 'my' people. And because one day, maybe, if I please you, you will take me away from this place."

"That cannot be," he said. "It would be so easy to lie to you, but I owe you too much for that."

"It doesn't matter," she said quietly. "Nothing matters, only that I may stay here with you, tonight."

21

"**W**HAT happened to you? What did you do? Tell us, everything," Lina said, her voice throaty with happiness, speaking to the children who sat before them cross-legged on the ground. Behind the kids, as the shadows of evening lengthened, was parked the old jeep the young man from Gumsa had given her. In it they had travelled about ten miles from the village, until the engine had boiled and they had decided to pull up for the night. Which left about the same distance, no more, to the sea. The sea, on the morrow, in the early morning. Ras Abu Khim, and the navy waiting, still waiting, offshore. It was still possible. It might seem like years but actually they had been held up at Askar for less than a week.

"They had donkeys, and camels,"

the little girl said eagerly —

" — and goats." The little boy.

"Yes, and goats too. We took them out every morning, to the fields, to the hillsides" — she waved her hands — "they were always wandering away and getting lost and then we had to find them." She frowned and shook her head, adding, "Sometimes we had to go miles and miles and it took all day."

"But, those people," Andersen said. "They looked after you, didn't they? Gave you food, and a place to sleep?"

"Oh yes," the little girl said. "They were quite nice really, though the food was very boring, always rice, always dates. But we like dates" — turning to her brother — "don't we?"

"You like them more than I do," the little boy said.

Not so 'little' any more, either, Andersen thought, watching him. Dressed now in a torn thobe and sandals he looked thinner, fined down, and his face more mature. Still a kid but a kid who had travelled some way, as they had all done, in the last seven days. He smiled less, was less eager to air his views, had no more questions, and had grown more self-assured. Different from the little girl, who had obviously burst out of the shell which had previously cocooned her, and who, just as obviously, had found a lot to enjoy in all that had happened to her, back there. He grimaced, watching them, giving thanks that at any rate they hadn't been mistreated, but thinking also that, in their different ways, the problems they posed would surely only get more complicated from now on. Still, he loved them, and was happy deep down to see them again.

"*He* got himself a girl-friend, in the village," the little girl said maliciously.

"He — *what*?" Lina cried, laughing.

"A little Arab girl called Leila," the little girl said, nodding. "But she was silly, I thought. She followed him around like a puppy."

The little boy stood up, blank-eyed,

and walked away, past the car, and into the trees. After a moment Andersen got up and followed him, hearing Lina say behind him, "You're becoming quite a little minx, aren't you. Haven't you two been getting on so well?" —

And the little girl in reply, "You have to keep him in his place, that's all. Otherwise he wants to boss everyone about all the time."

Some fifty yards into the bush, the little boy had come to a halt, at the edge of a wide sandy gully. Now leaned against the trunk of a half-grown casuarina, staring steadily at a pebble in his hand. He didn't look up when Andersen approached and settled down on his haunches a yard or two away. The father-son counselling bit was a role he had never played before and he racked his brains for a commonplace way to begin. But finally the boy saved him the trouble.

"I hated it, back there in the village," he said. He looked round, stared at Andersen, his eyes dark and half-closed.

"They were like animals, and lived like pigs. There were six boys, and we all slept in the same bed, on the floor."

"Half the world lives in much the same way," Andersen said quietly, and then wished he hadn't, catching a look, of disappointment, in the boy's eyes. "What I mean is," he went on, "apart from that sort of thing, they were good people, weren't they? They weren't cruel, or unkind?"

"They fingered me, touched me, and they smelt," the little boy said.

"Arabs are like that, they do 'touch' one another a lot. It's their way of showing they're friends — "

"They touched me *here*," the little boy snapped, indicating his groin.

Andersen screwed up his eyes and shook his head, searching for words, the right words if possible, if such existed. Could find none for the moment, so got up and went to the boy; halted close beside him. Looked down at his hands and asked, "Did they, hurt you, in any way?"

288

"No, I wouldn't let them. I fought them. I spat at them."

"Good for you."

"Not good for me. They laughed at me and put crawlies in my food."

"Who did? Boys, or men?"

"Boys. Big boys. But one of the men, I think, he was egging them on."

"Bastards!" Andersen said.

"But, what did they want?" the little boy asked curiously, looking round and up into Andersen's face. He shook his head. "Something dirty, I know that, but what?"

To tell, or not to tell, Andersen wondered, to tell now — and darkness nearly upon them — or postpone it, until he had spoken with Lina and got her advice, until the little boy was a year or two older. Surely it would be better to tell now, when what had happened was uppermost in the boy's mind and clawing at his thoughts, but maybe *not*, for that very same reason. Surely, surely, this 'son' of his was still too young? Better another time, another place, when he himself was better prepared.

As he hesitated, frowning, the little boy said accusingly, "You're not going to tell me, are you?"

In the end he funked it. "I will, Michael, I promise you, and quite soon," he said. He reached out a hand to touch the boy, but then didn't. "Leave it be now, will you do that? Please, I'd rather . . ."

"I thought you wouldn't tell me," the little boy said. He stared at Andersen balefully for a moment; then turned his back and stalked away.

★ ★ ★

"The back, how is it?" she asked. They lay together in the dark, under the stars, some distance from 'camp', touching, feeling their way towards one another again. In a little while they would make love, he thought, when they were ready for it and it could not be held back any longer. But, if and when they did, perhaps she would smell the tang of Aisha's sweat on his body, and what then?

"It itches and aches," he said, "but it's getting better all the time."

"My poor darling. I'll look at it in the morning." Then, "Was it an old woman who doctored you, back there? The same one who came to me? She seemed to know very well what she was doing."

"Not an old woman, a young girl," Andersen said noncommittally. "I think . . . I think she was the old woman's pupil. She mentioned her once."

"They know many things, old remedies, that we don't," Lina said.

After a few moments, his hand gently caressing her flank, he said quietly, "And thee, Lin', what was it like for you? They beat you, didn't they? That's why the old woman came — "

"I don't want to think about it!" she said harshly, and tensed. Then, relaxing slowly until she began to tremble, whispered, "Sometime I will

291

have to tell you, or you will find out — you will perceive it in me — so I better tell you now."

"Tell me what?"

"He raped me, that man from Gumsa — Ali, his name is. He raped me several times. That's why he gave us the jeep, the food, the water."

All he said was, "I knew, it was likely. My love, it's unimportant, so long as you're all right."

"No, it's *not* unimportant!" she said bitterly. "You don't understand, the half of it. Maybe it's better you don't, but I have to tell you, so that you know, about me . . . It's my penance, to tell you," she added.

"Don't!" he cried. "Please! — don't."

"You would rather not know?" — curiously.

"I would rather not know," he agreed. Then, at her silence, "Because, if you tell me, then I must also tell you, something, and I'd rather not do that."

She hugged him to her then, forgetful

for a moment of the state of his back. He drew breath sharply as pain took him, and she gasped, shaking her head in contrition. "I love you so much, that is all," she whispered, her voice breaking. "There *is* nothing else."

"And I love you. You're the whole world to me. *Nothing* can alter that."

"But I have shamed you, and shamed myself."

"It happens. But all we can do is, live with it, isn't that so?"

"Yes," she said. "Yes."

But they did not make love that night. They slept, when they slept, very close, but without making love.

22

IN the morning, early, the jeep's engine would not start. They waited, cursing their luck, for the damp and mists of morning to clear: thinking that moisture had very likely got into the points, the plugs, the terminals, and that she would not start for that reason. But even after the sun had risen and warmed everything up, she would not go, and soon enough the battery began to die and the starter-motor to churn agonizingly, with their renewed efforts. So, before the battery failed altogether, they tried to push-start her, get her going that way, again without success. For some reason unknown to them the engine refused to catch, and their desperate shoving merely exhausted them.

And all the time Ras Abu Khim was no more than ten miles away, not far over the horizon, at the end of the dirt trail to the sea. The thought of that unknown place, so often pictured in their minds — a headland and the ocean beyond, and a ship out there — tormented their thoughts. So near, Jesus, so near.

They rested in the shade for a while, in silence; drank water, and slowly recovered their strength and will. Andersen had a last look under the bonnet of the old jeep and tried everything they knew to coax life out of the rusted engine. When that last hope also failed, they set off, openly, down the trail, carrying their bottles of water and what food they had left with them. They would march for two hours, they decided, rest up at a suitable spot, if they could find one, through the heat of the day, and hope to make it to the sea by sundown. Conceivably, if they stuck to the trail, someone might happen by and give them a lift. Conceivably, for there were other possibilities also, but those were risks they were prepared to take.

Desert now, empty, treeless: they had come down from the hills into the waterless plain that skirted the coast for hundreds of miles in this section of the country. Occasionally there were patches of camel-thorn, occasionally low 'dunes', but not the slightest sign of habitation of any kind, not even the abandoned shelters of the Bedouin. The weight and ferocity of the sun gradually increased until the sweat coursed from their bodies, and after a time he and Lina tore strips off the thobes they were wearing to contrive makeshift turbans for them all. Nevertheless, after little more than an hour of marching they were spent and had to rest, lying face-down at the trail-side, passing one of the three bottles of water left one to the other: hot, strong-tasting water from the wells of Askar that did little to quench their thirst.

For the first time then, since leaving

the village, he became really afraid. In a way subtly different from ever before. He looked into Lina's eyes as she raised her head beside him to catch his, and became aware that the same fear was in her too. Not of death, or even terrible suffering, which had been with them from the beginning, but of dying *like this*, their bodies scorched to shambling weakness in some nameless and burning wasteland when, not far away, only a little further, just beyond their reach, lay safety. Surely, safety? It seemed a travesty of life, their lives together, to die like this. Not for them, *it could not be*, to die, as pitiably as countless others had done, when their goal was but 'a few steps' away. Yet the prospect was only too real now.

He staggered to his feet, stood swaying, a wave of faintness almost overwhelming him. Closed his eyes tight until his head cleared, and then looked around: back along the trail, out over the desert, his body turning as his eyes searched fruitlessly, into the shimmering distances, trying to pick out anything that moved, anything at all 'different'. But there was nothing and he looked down, caught Lina's eyes again, as she looked up at him, and shook his head.

She rose to her feet, automatically dusting down the tattered garment she wore, and then called the children by name — her voice unrecognisable — gesturing with her hands for them to get up as well. When they had done so, she said, "We drink all we want, now, all that's left — and then walk on, as far as we can go."

"Yes," Andersen said.

★ ★ ★

The three men came upon them unawares. Dark, bearded, their heads muffled, they appeared out of the desert and approached . . . It was long past midday, Lina, Andersen and the kids had marched as far as they could, until they could go no further; then, with the last of their strength, had dug hollows for themselves in the sand, and burrowed into them, covering their heads, and any other exposed parts of their bodies, with cloths and dust. There they lay, fighting for breath in the crucifying heat, mouths gaping, in a state bordering on coma, to wait until evening. Knowing in their hearts that they had little chance of lasting that long.

The little boy lay beside Andersen, his body close, taking a little shelter from that of the man. One of the intruders came forward, reached down and picked him up easily in his arms and went back to rejoin his companions, one of whom held the boy's reeling head while the man who had picked him up poured water over his face and down his throat from a canteen. This done the man set him down on the sand, squatted down beside him and rested a hand on the boy's shoulder.

A second man came forward, took

up the little girl from Lina's side, retreated; gave her water also; smiling and making clicking noises with his tongue as the little girl choked and moaned and struggled weakly in his arms.

Sitting up, Andersen had watched, his vision blurred, his brain registering only dimly what he saw. Seeing men — three men — armed, two of them, with rifles: men from where? — and the children now in their hands, being given water, given life. He turned his head and Lina was watching also, a yard or two away, her face lifted and a mask of sweat and dirt, one hand outstretched on the sand opening, closing, as though of its own accord. As consciousness returned to him, he called out, to the three men, his voice little better than a croak, "What you want?"

"These children," the leader said shortly. "We take them now. With us they will live."

"No!"

But from where she lay Lina made some despairing sound, which stopped him, and he stared at her again, questioningly.

"Take them!" Her voice suddenly clear: strident, anguished, but clear. "Yes, take them! Look after them!" She raised her head, accusing, supplicating. "They are yours, but may God *curse* you if they come to harm."

"We do not harm them, mother," the man said.

"Then take them!"

"Water. Give us *water*," Andersen begged.

"We have no water for you," the man said. He looked round at his two companions, and the man who had stayed beside the little boy stood up, lifting the boy like a sack and dumping him over his shoulder. Then the three of them turned their backs and walked away. Disappeared once again, in a minute or two, into the distance, the shimmering haze. Only when they had gone did it dawn upon Andersen that he had seen one of the men before, the leader: he had seen him at Gumsa. Not from Askar, those three.

She crawled to him, and he put his arm about her shoulders. In silence they sat for several seconds, bereft, heads down. He turned her to him, his free hand in her hair, and she collapsed against him, but could not weep. Eventually she reached up blindly and touched his cheek. He gripped her with all the strength he had left, tried to speak, but then stopped —

One of the men was coming back. He approached with the long confident stride of the Bedouin, until he was twenty yards from them. Then he bent and placed on the sand first a canteen of water and then, taking it from his belt, a knife which he set down beside the canteen. After that he looked up, at them.

"In payment," he said simply. He raised a hand in farewell, turned, and strode away.

23

THEY came to Ras Abu Khim in the early hours of the morning. There was no promontory, merely a long rocky tongue of land jutting a few hundred yards out into the ocean. The 'road' ran all the way out to the point, where there had once been a jetty whose salt-encrusted piles still stuck up in two lines above the surface of the water. They could see many miles along the shoreline both to left and right of them — east and west — but there was no sign of a village or habitation of any kind. Out to sea there was no sign of a vessel, either, not close in to shore nor hull-down on the horizon. Of course not, after all this time.

Nevertheless, that they had come so far, had endured the hardships and sufferings of the past weeks, for *nothing*, took time to sink in. They sat, shoulders touching, arms about their knees, looking out over the water, scanning the horizon until their eyes ached, until gradually acceptance — very bitter, very saddening, of failure — filled their minds to the exclusion of all else. This was the end. They were alone and had nothing, their canteen was empty, and the few seabirds they could see, gulls, cormorants, if by any remote chance they could snare them, were inedible. Behind them was a hostile land, and to go on, a bit further, along the coast, in one direction or the other, was now beyond them. They did not have the will, never mind the strength, left. So death, a savage pitiless death, in a few hours.

"I'm sorry, so sorry," he said, and put his head down on his knees.

She got to her feet and went down to the water, stripped off her thobe, and waded out, all her movements accomplished slowly, painfully, and with concentration. Waded further out, until the water came up to her waist. Her body, though terribly thin, was still lovely, when you couldn't see the ulcers on her legs; her face, as she turned to look about her, was still vital and exciting to him — though hollow-eyed, haggard, and prematurely aged — when you couldn't see the running sores round her mouth and the broken sun-blisters on her cheeks. He thought to call out to her, to warn her that what she was doing was madness, to bathe in salt water in the dehydrated state she was in; but then didn't call out, because that didn't matter any more. She ducked her head under water, washed slowly but comprehensively, hair face and body, even swam a few strokes, and then waded ashore again. Returned to where he sat, her garment over her shoulder. "I thought there might be crabs," she said. "But there aren't any, not around here. Maybe — ?"

She stood over him, but did not go on, and when he looked up he saw she was staring over his shoulder, at something a little way off. Then, without speaking further, she moved round him and, as he turned to follow her with his eyes, walked fifteen or twenty yards; then halted again, staring fixedly at something on the ground. After a moment she called, "Jack! Jack, come here. Look at this!" Quickly and without thinking she shook out the garment she had been carrying and shrugged into it, her eyes never leaving what she was looking at.

A Union Flag, roughly daubed in white paint on a flat rock, perhaps twelve inches by eight, and under it, also in white, letters and number W32 S12. Whenever it had been done, one thing was certain: it hadn't been done many days ago.

He stood beside her, breathing through his mouth, his mind refusing to function, merely taking it in.

"What does it mean?" she asked, her

eyes wide, incredulous, as she turned to him.

He shook his head. Then said slowly, as if surfacing from sleep, "'W' — west, 'S' — south. Perhaps?"

"32 what? 12 what?"

"Yards, miles — "

"Paces!" she said. "Paces!"

"Let us try," he said. "Which way is west?"

"That way." She whirled, stared down the trail leading to the spot on which they stood.

He took up position beside the rock on which the Union Flag was painted, and started to pace it out, taking big strides, counting out loud. " . . . 32." At the trailside was a blaze of white on another stone.

"South twelve," he said, and turned in that direction. With her just behind him, at his shoulder, he walked twelve paces. Nothing. No blaze this time, only rocks, many of them, loose-lying, flat to the ground. Bending down, going from one to the other, scurrying, they turned them over. And eventually found it, a small package wrapped in oilcloth.

He unwrapped it, breathing hard, his hands clumsy and shaking. A cigarette-tin, — Senior Service, 50 — and inside a single sheet of paper, folded. He unfolded it and held it up so that they could both read. The message was typewritten, and said:-

'Aboard HM Fleet Auxiliary 'Lindis-farne', 1600 hrs, 10.8.8–, vicinity Ras Abu Khim. We are instructed to break off vigil now on approach of national frigate, possibly hostile. We will return, all being well, one fortnight from today, on Monday 24.8.8–, and will be in position off Ras Abu Khim point by 2100 hrs, flashing red, green, red, at ten minute intervals through the night. Using 'Tundra 16' torch we have left you you should reply in same way, and a boat will come in to take you off. Supplies have been left you at following location: North, five hundred and sixteen yards from spot in which this letter was deposited, dune on shoreline with slab of bedrock jutting out at waist height; under slab there is opening to small 'cave' which we have blocked in, hopefully leaving no traces, with sacking and sand. There.

Hold on. We have not forgotten you. We will be back. Signed: Tom Rogers, Lt. Commander RN'

"What day is it today?" she asked anxiously.

"I've no idea," he said, and shook his head. "Nor of the date."

★ ★ ★

They found the cache of supplies easily enough, but what it comprised took their breath away. There was water, gallons and gallons of it, in four-gallon plastic containers; there was tinned food, corned beef, ham, tongue;

potatoes, tomatoes, green vegetables, fruit; there was tea, coffee, sugar, milk; there was a primus stove, four gallons of kerosene; there were blankets, medicines, torches, candles; two two-man tents and groundsheets; there was a rifle, a Weber .256 plus a hundred rounds of ammunition; there was fishing-line, hooks, sinkers; there were two bottles of whisky, half a dozen well-thumbed paperbacks and four cartons of cigarettes. After they had discovered the full extent of what had been left them, and while they were slaking their raging thirst, Lina broke down and wept, sitting on the sand above the beach, her head in her hands, the hole of the 'cave' under the slab gaping behind them. He knew that the emotion she could no longer contain was partly in mourning for the fact that the children were no longer with them — had not made it this far — and held her to him in silence until she had cried herself out.

But he knew also that now they

had to plan, and act, fairly quickly: that on this beach of theirs they were probably safe during the heat of the day, but not safe, not safe at all, in the cool of evening, at night, and during the hours of daylight before the sun's heat battened upon the land. Sooner or later, if he read matters correctly, someone — a party of men — would come looking for them, expecting to find their bodies, so that they might report back on their deaths.

Together they worked it out as best they could, how many days it had been since their departure from Ayoun, and racked their brains until they were fairly certain of the day and date when the attack on the camp had taken place. By computation then, and with reference again to Tom Rogers' letter, they had eight days to wait before the navy came back: eight days or, to be quite certain, they should be in readiness from the night of the seventh day. So, seven days, but wait, live, where? Not here, there was not room enough in the little cave both for their supplies and themselves. Better by far to 'live' somewhere else, if they could find somewhere secluded to pitch a tent, not far away; keep their cache of supplies hidden and return to it only when they needed to, blotting out all traces, as best they might, of their coming and going.

After a breakfast of ham and tomatoes and *hot sweet tea*, they set off along the beach, to look for the sort of place they needed. And found it, as good a place as any, within a quarter of a mile of the cave. A long narrow gully, a dry wash that sloped gently down from the slightly higher desert plain to the beach, cut between five-foot walls of packed sand by a million years of infrequent rains. Once in this gully, at its lower end, and as long as they kept their heads down they, and their tent, would be virtually invisible from the landward side. It was unthinkable that they might find anywhere better, and they gave up their search immediately.

For the next two hours, in blazing heat but uncaring, worked to set up their campsite under one wall of the gully, transferring there from the cave everything that they immediately needed and could conceivably use. And then with painstaking care blocked up the mouth of the cave again and, using their hands, cloths, blankets, retraced their path to their campsite effacing all sign of their passing to and fro. When they had done that they were totally exhausted, ill with weariness and heat, half dead, and passed out in their tent for the rest of that day.

24

THE next three days were the calmest, most beautiful, they ever spent together. Gradually they were able to put the thought of the children, and their fate, out of their minds; very quickly, with good food, with bathing in the sea, with the medicines that had been left them, their bodies healed, filled out, and recovered their strength. Of course they were wary at all times, of course they were anxious occasionally, of course they had vile dreams and bouts of sadness, but for the most part they *knew* that nothing could go wrong now, that their period of desperate travail was over, that in due course of time they would be picked up and would be able to resume lives which bore some resemblance to the normality they had once known.

Not unchanged, of course not. They were different beings now from the two 'novices' who had made their decisions that day at Ayoun, and looked very different, older, harder, more cynical, and their attitude to the world had changed. They cared for no one but themselves, had lost what little idealism they may have once possessed, and meant — they didn't admit to this but it was implicit in the plans they made for the future — to screw the world for all they could get out of it, and ruthlessly protect their own interests, for however much longer (many, many years, they hoped) they had left to them.

But, on the evening of their fourth night at Ras Abu Khim, Andersen fell sick. They had had a lovely day, walking for miles in the early morning along the shore, collecting shells, watching the sea-birds migrating north, swimming, making love with tenderness and quiet passion, playing a game of their own devising with pebbles on a small 'court' they marked out on the sand; had eaten well and slept long hours in their tent during the heat of the day; had opened up their cache of supplies in late afternoon and spent a delightful half-hour sorting out 'goodies' to supplement those they already had at their campsite. When they were done and had covered their tracks again, they were weary, drenched with togetherness and pleasure and, in the last of the daylight, sat outside their tent, backs to the sand-wall beside it, and commenced their already well-established ritual of 'talk' and a couple of quiet whiskies before supper.

But, after a time, Andersen put down his plastic 'glass', frowned, and raised a hand to his forehead. Said quietly, "Hell, I've got a headache."

"Too much sun?" she said.

"Mm, probably. I'd better take a couple of pills." He got a little shakily to his feet, then bent double and went inside the tent.

She heard him scrabbling about in

there, searching for Panadol or codeine that they kept with the other medical supplies beyond their bedding and pillows; then there was silence and he didn't come out again.

After a time she called, "What are you doing?"

No answer, and she crawled quickly to the tent-fly and looked within. Could see little and felt around with her hand for the torch they kept ready just within the entrance. Found it and snapped it on.

He lay spreadeagled on their blankets, face down, breathing heavily through his mouth. As she went to him suddenly he rolled over and sat up, fought his way past her, groaning, and crawled outside. Staggered a little way down the wash, holding his stomach; then squatted, gathered his thobe in his hands, and vacated his bowels. When it was over, turned to her, his face drained, glistening with sweat, and muttered, "Sorry, I — I couldn't hold it." Finally, falling forward on hand

and knees he was comprehensively sick, retching, heaving, wiping his mouth with the back of his wrist. Began weakly, after that, to brush sand with one hand over the mess he had made.

"What is it?" she asked. "What can I get you?"

"Don't know!" He knelt on the sand, head back now, taking deep shuddering breaths.

She went to him and when he staggered to his feet again bent and put his arm about her shoulders. Got him back to the tent and inside, and made him lie down. "Chloromycetin," he said hoarsely. "Try that. But it can't be. I've had my shots."

So, using the torch, but her hands shaking despite her efforts at control, she found chloromycetin in their medical kit, got him to take a couple of big pills with water. To no avail, he couldn't keep them down and barely made it to the tent-fly before vomiting again. And so it went on, through the night:

his stomach rejected anything given it within seconds, the dysentery, or whatever it was, recurred at frequent intervals, and gradually his pain became so intense, and he became so weak, that he could not make it outside even with her help. By midnight he lay comatose, in his own filth, fevered and mumbling to himself, and she knew nothing else to do for him but to keep cold compresses always fresh and apply them to his forehead and cheeks; clean his body and bedding with wet towels from time to time. Listening, when sometimes his ravings became louder and more coherent, to one-sided conversations he held in his mind with someone called Aisha, a girl, with whom he had once been intimate and for whose fate, whatever that was or had been, he held himself at least partly to blame . . .

But by the early hours of the morning she was exhausted herself and could continue no longer. Wrapped herself in blankets outside the tent and, despite the feelings of fear and inadequacy that tormented her, managed to snatch a few hours sleep. Praying that somehow, by some miracle, he would be better in the morning, that his great physical strength and long experience of tropical climes — his built up immunity to diseases endemic to them — might eventually pull him through.

But they did not. Gradually, through the next morning, he grew weaker, more emaciated and, though his fever lessened, then vanished altogether, the only result seemed to be that his pallor became more pronounced, his breathing began to falter until his face became a mask of death. Everything she could think of she had tried: dragging him out of the tent to give him 'fresh' air, made him a concoction of kaolin and boiled rice and forced some of it down his throat; talked to him, cajoled him, *cursed* him, trying somehow to get through to him, make him react and fight back. Without perceptible result, and by midday she was certain he was dead.

★ ★ ★

She had taken leave of him: holding his body across her lap and hugging him to her from time to time, staring down into his face, stroking his hair; and then quickly had pressed the eyelids together over his eyes. After that, still dry-eyed herself, moving in a daze but all her actions purposeful and without apparent pause for thought, had buried him, in the sand, not ten yards from the tent. Then she had cleaned up, herself and her clothing, by bathing in the sea, his bedding and anything else he might have recently touched by scrubbing it in sea water and using carbolic soap. Then, while everything dried in the sun, she had taken down the tent and resited it further down the wash —

Sat now, late afternoon, with her back against the sand-wall not two yards from the tent-fly, and let her mind wander, taking up and sipping from a glass a third full of neat whisky from time to time —

"Woman, you are alone." She looked up, into the cloudless blue of the sky, then took out and lit a cigarette from the packet on the sand at her side. "Your man is gone, but you are still here. First your children were taken from you, and now your man . . . Who did this to you, and how did it happen? Who shall *pay*, besides yourself? Yes, *pay*, because this did not have to happen, neither the loss of your children nor his death. They say that things are 'written' — merde! Cowards, those who believe that! — in this world there is always a culprit: the possibility, the *necessity*, for retribution. While life remains. That is what we are *for*, those that are left — "

So the Arab in her, after all these years.

"He was a good man, a brave man — *mine*. As men go he was the beginning and the end, an exciting lover, an easy-going companion, in good times; in others devoted, a 'giver', and never sought to make me other than what I am . . . "

She wept then, for the first time since his death: slumped forward, her head hanging between her knees, letting everything go. When she had recovered, after a few minutes, sat back, a darkness, of longing, in her mind.

'Can I live without him, do I want to? An extraordinary thought such as, no more than a month ago, I would have dismissed from my mind out of hand of course I would have wanted to live, then; in any conceivable circumstances, then. Now? Not now. All the plans we made, sitting here on this beach in the twilight, but a day or two ago, are meaningless, now. I do not remember what I was, before him; all I know is that I cannot be what I was again. And if I do not want that, now he has gone, then there is nothing that I want. Except retribution. That is all that remains, and somehow I will contrive it. I *will*. I *owe* that to him. And my children.'

After a time she went to the tent and got out the rifle. Found a small can of oil among their supplies, and settled down to clean it, and by so doing familiarise herself with its mechanism.

25

SEIFUDDIN came down into Askar by jeep, bringing four of his closest retainers with him. He made such 'inspections' from time to time. As usual the villagers vacated one of their best houses for him in the centre of the village, and it was there that he set up his 'court'. He spent several days, hearing pleas, solving disputes, dispensing justice of a traditional kind, all the time listening to the reports of spies and informers as they came in. By the time four days were up he knew pretty well what had happened in the case of the two faranji and their children who had 'passed through' the village some days back, and took steps accordingly.

Ali, the young man from Gumsa, who had been one of his own henchmen — originally from Kamil, but from a family without significance — he had castrated, left without medical attention of any kind, so that he died within twelve hours of the deed being done. Aisha, the young girl, he sent for, but she had fled. He had her pursued and brought back, gave her to his men for their entertainment, and she was never seen again. The case of the Bedouin who had given water to the two fugitives after their escape from the village, however, was a little different, and he held his hand for a time. The man came from a tribe of nomads, tough independent people with long memories who feared no man on earth, and no member of that tribe might be so summarily dealt with. After a while he thought of a way. He gave a feast, as was incumbent upon him so to do during the course of his stay in the village, to which the man was 'invited': that is to say, expected to come. At that feast a certain potion, not known in those parts, but used sometimes in the interior of the country, was introduced into his food. With no immediate effect. The man would remain in good health for a month, perhaps longer, but would eventually die in agony, his insides eaten away by cancerous growths. Thus did he, Seifuddin, settle up with those who had crossed him.

After he had done so, and as soon as other and more important business would permit, he turned his attention to the two faranji themselves. Apparently they were still there, at Ras Abu Khim; apparently, so it was reported to him, they still survived. How? An extraordinary thing. They were not Bedu whose knowledge of the desert and the fleeting sustenance it sometimes threw up was inborn, whose 'feel' and 'scent' for underground water defied all logic. They were not fisherfolk — as far as he knew — to garner the bare elements of survival from the sea with their bare hands. And yet, they were still there, the woman anyway, for the man had not been seen for some time. Strange faranji then, perhaps, and more worthy of respect than any he had ever met or heard of.

Now they had begun to light a big fire every night above the beach down there: its blaze could be seen in the distance from the hills above the village . . .

★ ★ ★

Her attitude to what she was setting out to do had become fatalistic: old age was upon her, she thought to herself sometimes, wryly. Since the night the navy had come back, had flashed their lights, and she had made no reply to them, she existed in a kind of limbo, waiting. He, Seifuddin, would come sooner or later, or He would not come, it was in the lap of the Unknown. She was ready, if He did, that was all.

If He came by night, she had little chance, she knew that; if He came during the heat of the day she had no chance at all: she had to sleep sometime. More likely, though, and in keeping with tradition and good sense, He would come either in the early morning or in the evening. At those times, well in advance of them in fact, she was in position and maintained constant vigilance.

There was a little depression, or fault in the land, two hundred yards inland and about the same distance from the tent. There. It was there she lay up, rifle, ammo, water to hand, the long knife which that Bedouin had given them taped to her thigh. It was only after the navy had been and gone, a night or two after, that the idea of a big fire had come to her, to draw Him to her. After that she spent an hour or two each day collecting driftwood, there was plenty of it around, and from then on spent her nights in the vicinity of the blaze, waiting.

But slowly, inexorably, the pattern of her existence began to take its toll. She became lightheaded occasionally, for three days fell sick of some nameless ailment and could not leave her tent, was afflicted in the damp cold nights by rheumatism and arthritis. Slowly too, certain elements of her once copious supplies began to run out and she was forced to ration herself, particularly of water. Gradually the fine edge of her anger and determination was ground down, diminished, adulterated, and she began to forget the reason for her self-imposed travail. Often she became too tired to collect wood and even when she had it forgot to light it, or didn't bother, preferring to sleep the night away. Gradually she began to take less care of herself, and lost her appetite, at first making some effort to force herself to eat but then, finding that she could manage with very little, gave up worrying about it. She became thin, emaciated, her fine body wasting away, her breasts were empty and dangled on her chest and once again she was plagued by sores and ulcers whose spread she did little to alleviate. She began constantly to talk to herself, reliving in her mind and giving utterance to feelings and experiences that were not of recent origin, of the time of Jack Andersen, but of her childhood and of the time, light-years past, when she had lived a life in Cambridge and London. In short she became old and a little mad. Finally, the savage heat and glare of the desert began to burn out the nerves of her eyes and her vision became hazy and lacking definition. She became afraid, lonely, and wished for her life to end, but did not have the courage or the will left to effect her own destruction.

* * *

He came then, one day in late afternoon, in a jeep with three others, all heavily armed. Found her wandering near her camp, staring at the ground and muttering to herself. He made the driver pull up when he was still fifty yards away — and as yet she had apparently neither seen nor heard them — and watched. She was stooped, her clothing in rags, and obviously unarmed. After a time he ordered his men to get out, approach her carefully, surround her, and bring her to him. He remained in the jeep.

She saw the men when they closed in on her, cried out, attempted to run, but was too weak to escape them. As they approached fell on her knees, raising her thin arms in supplication; then bowed her head to the sand and hid her face from them. As they halted beside her and looked down at her, they could see that she was shaking in terror, filthy, unkempt, and exchanged glances, of pity and distaste.

Two of them lifted her to her feet and between them — the third man bringing up the rear — forced her to walk, half-dragging her, in the direction of the jeep. She struggled, ineffectually, whining and crying out, shaking her head from side to side, and tears trickled down her cheeks. When they reached the jeep, they released her, and she fell forward, prostrated herself once again, and covered her head with her hands.

Seifuddin got down then and came closer, motioning his minions back. Lined, aged hawk-faced expressionless, he eyed her, what was left of her, and then said, "Do you know who I am?"

She raised her head, mouth open, chin trembling, and nodded several times, but did not look at him. Said indistinctly, abjectly, "Master, have mercy. Have mercy upon me."

He stared at her a moment or two longer, a grim smile thinning his mouth, his good eye half-closed. Then said to his men, "Put her in the jeep. We will take her back to Askar and find a family to look after her. Let her end her days in peace."

THE END

WITH SOMEBODY ELSE
Theresa Charles

Rosamond sets off for Cornwall with Hugo to meet his family, blissfully unaware of the shocks in store for her.

A SUMMER FOR STRANGERS
Claire Hamilton

Because she had lost her job, her flat and she had no money, Tabitha agreed to pose as Adam's future wife although she believed the scheme to be deceitful and cruel.

VILLA OF SINGING WATER
Angela Petron

The disquieting incidents that occurred at the Vatican and the Colosseum did not trouble Jan at first, but then they became increasingly unpleasant and alarming.

DOCTOR NAPIER'S NURSE
Pauline Ash

When cousins Midge and Derry are entered as probationer nurses on the same day but at different hospitals they agree to exchange identities.

A GIRL LIKE JULIE
Louise Ellis

Caroline absolutely adored Hugh Barrington, but then Julie Crane came into their lives. Julie was the kind of girl who attracts men without even trying.

COUNTRY DOCTOR
Paula Lindsay

When Evan Richmond bought a practice in a remote country village he did not realise that a casual encounter would lead to the loss of his heart.

ENCORE
Helga Moray

Craig and Janet realise that their true happiness lies with each other, but it is only under traumatic circumstances that they can be reunited.

NICOLETTE
Ivy Preston

When Grant Alston came back into her life, Nicolette was faced with a dilemma. Should she follow the path of duty or the path of love?

THE GOLDEN PUMA
Margaret Way

Catherine's time was spent looking after her father's Queensland farm. But what life was there without David, who wasn't interested in her?

HOSPITAL BY THE LAKE
Anne Durham

Nurse Marguerite Ingleby was always ready to become personally involved with her patients, to the despair of Brian Field, the Senior Surgical Registrar, who loved her.

VALLEY OF CONFLICT
David Farrell

Isolated in a hostel in the French Alps, Ann Russell sees her fiancé being seduced by a young girl. Then comes the avalanche that imperils their lives.

NURSE'S CHOICE
Peggy Gaddis

A proposal of marriage from the incredibly handsome and wealthy Reagan was enough to upset any girl — and Brooke Martin was no exception.

A DANGEROUS MAN
Anne Goring

Photographer Polly Burton was on safari in Mombasa when she met enigmatic Leon Hammond. But unpredictability was the name of the game where Leon was concerned.

PRECIOUS INHERITANCE
Joan Moules

Karen's new life working for an authoress took her from Sussex to a foreign airstrip and a kidnapping; to a real life adventure as gripping as any in the books she typed.

VISION OF LOVE
Grace Richmond

When Kathy takes over the rundown country kennels she finds Alec Stinton, a local vet, very helpful. But their friendship arouses bitter jealousy and a tragedy seems inevitable.

CRUSADING NURSE
Jane Converse

It was handsome Dr. Corbett who opened Nurse Susan Leighton's eyes and who set her off on a lonely crusade against some powerful enemies and a shattering struggle against the man she loved.

WILD ENCHANTMENT
Christina Green

Rowan's agreeable new boss had a dream of creating a famous perfume using her precious Silverstar, but Rowan's plans were very different.

DESERT ROMANCE
Irene Ord

Sally agrees to take her sister Pam's place as La Chartreuse the dancer, but she finds out there is more to it than dyeing her hair red and looking like her sister.

HEART OF ICE
Marie Sidney

How was January to know that not only would the warmth of the Swiss people thaw out her frozen heart, but that she too would play her part in helping someone to live again?

LUCKY IN LOVE
Margaret Wood

Companion-secretary to wealthy gambler Laura Duxford, who lived in Monaco, seemed to Melanie a fabulous job. Especially as Melanie had already lost her heart to Laura's son, Julian.

NURSE TO PRINCESS JASMINE
Lilian Woodward

Nick's surgeon brother, Tom, performs an operation on an Arabian princess, and she invites Tom, Nick and his fiancé to Omander, where a web of deceit and intrigue closes about them.

THE WAYWARD HEART
Eileen Barry

Disaster-prone Katherine's nickname was "Kate Calamity", but her boss went too far with an outrageous proposal, which because of her latest disaster, she could not refuse.

FOUR WEEKS IN WINTER
Jane Donnelly

Tessa wasn't looking forward to meeting Paul Mellor again — she had made a fool of herself over him once before. But was Orme Jared's solution to her problem likely to be the right one?

SURGERY BY THE SEA
Sheila Douglas

Medical student Meg hadn't really wanted to go and work with a G.P. on the Welsh coast although the job had its compensations. But Owen Roberts was certainly not one of them!

HEAVEN IS HIGH
Anne Hampson

The new heir to the Manor of Marbeck had been found. But it was rather unfortunate that when he arrived unexpectedly he found an uninvited guest, complete with stetson and high boots.

LOVE WILL COME
Sarah Devon

June Baker's boss was not really her idea of her ideal man, but when she went from third typist to boss's secretary overnight she began to change her mind.

ESCAPE TO ROMANCE
Kay Winchester

Oliver and Jean first met on Swale Island. They were both trying to begin their lives afresh, but neither had bargained for complications from the past.

CASTLE IN THE SUN
Cora Mayne

Emma's invalid sister, Kym, needed a warm climate, and Emma jumped at the chance of a job on a Mediterranean island. But Emma soon finds that intrigues and hazards lurk on the sunlit isle.

BEWARE OF LOVE
Kay Winchester

Carol Brampton resumes her nursing career when her family is killed in a car accident. With Dr. Patrick Farrell she begins to pick up the pieces of her life, but is bitterly hurt when insinuations are made about her to Patrick.

DARLING REBEL
Sarah Devon

When Jason Farradale's secretary met with an accident, her glamorous stand-in was quite unable to deal with one problem in particular.